# CODE NAME: SERENDIPITY

**AMBER SMITH**

RAZORBILL

# RAZORBILL

An imprint of Penguin Random House LLC, New York

First published in the United States of America by Razorbill,
an imprint of Penguin Random House LLC, 2022

LIBRARY OF CONGRESS CATALOGING-IN-PUBLICATION DATA
Names: Smith, Amber, 1982– author.
Title: Code name: serendipity / Amber Smith.
Description: New York : Razorbill, 2022. | Audience: Ages 8–12 years
Summary: Eleven-year-old Sadie Mitchell-Rosen is having trouble fitting in at school
and at home, so when she meets a dog named Dewey things seem to get better for her.
Identifiers: LCCN 2021034711 | ISBN 9780593204917 (hardcover)
ISBN 9780593204931 (trade paperback) | ISBN 9780593204924 (ebook)
Subjects: CYAC: Coming of age—Fiction. | Self esteem—Fiction.
Human-animal relationships—Fiction. | Dogs—Fiction.
Classification: LCC PZ7.1.S595 Co 2022 | DDC [Fic]—dc23
LC record available at https://lccn.loc.gov/2021034711

Manufactured in Canada

1 3 5 7 9 10 8 6 4 2

FRI

Design by Rebecca Aidlin
Text set in Carre Noir Std

**For Darwin**

# Part One

# A HOWL IN THE WOODS

## Chapter 1

# THINGS THAT DON'T SUCK, LIKE FRENCH TOAST AND WEEKENDS

I'm always the first one to wake up on Sundays because it is my favorite day, and I never want to lose any time on the weekend by spending it asleep. Weekends mean no school. No math. No waiting, friendless, at the bus stop morning after morning. Weekends mean I get to video chat with my best friend, Jude, who just moved to Utah, and I get to help my moms make a big Sunday-morning breakfast. Weekends mean I can pretend things are still easy, the way they were before I turned eleven a few months ago.

Today is no different.

I hop out of bed and stick my feet into my frog slippers—which ribbit if I step hard enough on the little buttons inside the stuffing-filled frog heads—and make my way downstairs to the kitchen. My slippers echo *ribbitribbit, ribbitribbit* with each step.

I start getting out all the pans and mixing bowls and ingredients we will need, lining them up on the kitchen counter: bread from the old wooden bread box; eggs, milk, and real butter—not the healthy fake butter that Mom hates but Mama always tries to get us to use instead—from the fridge; vanilla extract and cinnamon and powdered sugar from the cupboard where we keep the spices; and Mama's vegetarian sausage patties from the freezer, because that is one food she won't negotiate on.

Sunday-morning breakfast is a family tradition. The best part is dipping the bread into the egg batter and then slapping it onto the hot skillet and listening to it sizzle. French toast is my favorite food of all time. I would eat it for every meal of every day if my moms would let me. But they won't. I've asked.

This is when Catniss Everdeen—my older brother Noah's cat—comes wandering into the kitchen sniffing around to see if she can steal anything. He named her after his favorite book character. I thought we should name her Purrmione Granger, but Moms said it was Noah's decision. Catniss is very good at creeping in and sneaking food when you're not looking. Once she walked off with a whole package of "faken," which is what Noah calls Mama's veggie bacon, and no one even noticed.

My moms usually come downstairs and start making their morning coffee by the time Catniss makes her way to the kitchen. So I sit on one of the stools at the counter and wait.

And I wait.

Catniss loses interest when she sees that no cooking is happening, and she curls up into a tiny cat-ball inside of the square of sunlight that shines through the window onto the kitchen floor.

Still no Moms.

My slippers *ribbitribbit* as I make my way back up the stairs, with Catniss leaping alongside me, swatting at my feet every few steps. I open my moms' bedroom door, expecting to find them sleeping in, only to discover the bed already made and my moms nowhere in sight.

"Moms?" I call out.

No answer.

I look everywhere—in the bathroom, behind the shower curtain, even in the closet—but the whole house is quiet.

Too quiet.

My heart starts to race as my mind scrolls through all of the terrible things that could have happened to my family: Abducted by aliens. Swallowed by a sinkhole. Trapped in an alternate universe that sucked in everyone in the world except for Catniss and me. Or maybe *I'm* the one who's stuck in an alternate universe!

"Moms!" I scream this time, struggling to breathe normally.

I hear Noah's bedroom door creak open in the hallway.

"Sadie, stop yelling," he says, with his eyes sleep-squinty and his big curly hair mushed up on one side of his head, flattened on the other. Catniss darts from Moms' bed and pounces on my left frog slipper, making it croak out a small *ribbit*, before she leaps inside Noah's room.

I let out the breath I've been holding, relieved to see him, because at least that rules out the whole alternate-universe thing. But I don't tell him that.

Instead, I ask, "Where are Moms?"

"Grandpa Ed's," he mumbles, and starts to go back to his room. "That means I'm in charge, and I say stop yelling and let me go back to sleep."

"But it's Sunday," I say. "And why didn't they ask if *I* wanted to come?"

I love when we visit Gramps. We always go to the park that's across the street from his apartment building and feed the pigeons and play checkers on this special table that's made out of two different colors of stone. Gramps likes to talk to everyone we see because he says they all have stories inside them. He even sees stories in me, and he always listens as I tell him all about the graphic novel I've been working on: *The Interstellar Adventures of S. Hawkins, Special Agent.* And he never forgets to ask about the progress of the fairy fortress—not fairy *garden*—that Jude and I created in the backyard way back when we were in second grade.

"Am I *Mom?*" Noah snaps at me, in that grumpy way he's been snapping at everyone lately. "How would I know?"

Noah just turned fourteen, which means he's in ninth grade this year. Now that he goes to a different school and takes a different bus than me, and has a girlfriend (even though he always says, "She's *a girl* who's my *friend*—not my *girlfriend*"), it's like he's decided to start acting like he's too cool to hang out with me. Or even be nice to me anymore. Which basically means he's turned into a total butthead.

"But what about breakfast?" I say, crossing my arms. "I already started getting everything set up."

"So?" he says with a shrug, pretending he doesn't know full well that Sunday-morning breakfast is a family tradition. "Just have cereal."

"Cereal?" I groan. "Cereal is for school days!"

"This is me caring." He rolls his eyes and closes his door in my face.

As if everything else wasn't already sucky enough, I'm really beginning to despise being the younger sibling. I used to love being the youngest. It made me feel special. But now that we're older it just feels like an excuse for everyone in my family to not take me seriously. I generally don't believe people should go around having archenemies and things like that, but if I had one, it would definitely be Noah.

So I knock as loud and hard as I can, pounding both of my fists against the door, and I don't stop until he opens it again.

"Leave me alone," he grumbles.

This time I walk away from him, saying loud enough to catch his attention, "I'm calling Moms!"

"Don't call them, Sadie," he says as he follows me down the stairs. "I'm serious; they're busy, and they don't need you annoying them right now!" I reach for the phone in the kitchen and start dialing, when Noah takes it away from me.

"Hey, butthead!" I yell at him. "Give that back to me. I'm telling Moms you're being mean."

"Don't be such a *toddler*!" That's his favorite thing to call me lately. "Moms didn't want me to tell you this because you're such a baby, but Grandpa Ed is—" He stops in the middle of his sentence.

"Gramps is what?" I ask.

"Gramps is . . . old, okay? Get a clue, buttmunch, they're not going for fun. They're going because he can't live alone anymore."

"Why not?" I ask, even though I'm not sure I want to know the answer.

Noah sighs and looks down. "The people at his apartment building called Mom because something happened in the middle of the night with Gramps being confused. He was wandering around the halls, or something weird like that." Noah pauses, and now even he looks a little worried, and he never seems worried about anything. "So Moms went there today to bring him back here."

"Maybe he was just sleepwalking?" I offer.

"He wasn't sleepwalking. He couldn't remember which apartment was his. Mom says he can't live alone anymore." He pulls down the boxes of cereal from the pantry, and I sit at the table. "I think he might have to go to a—" But he stops talking.

"To a what?" I ask when he doesn't finish. "Where does he have to go?"

"Never mind. Just don't tell Moms I told you about Gramps, okay?" he says, a little bit nicer—more like the way he used to talk to me—even if there is something he's not telling me. "They want to explain it all to you later."

Noah takes his bowl of cereal into the living room and turns on the TV.

Suddenly, the air in the kitchen feels strange and sticky and weird. Not at all like what a Sunday is supposed to feel like. I spoon my lumpy, soggy cereal to my mouth, but I'm not hungry anymore.

## Chapter 2

# BIFFLES AND PUZZLES

I go to my room and open my laptop to send Jude a message.

> ME: jude, r u around? can u video chat w/me?

> ME: it's a v strange day. just found out there might be something wrong with gramps. noah wouldn't tell me much. but moms left early this morning (before french toast even) to see gramps. im kinda freaking out . . .

I wait for a response.

> ME: i need a distraction. how was ur week? how'd ur science fair volcano turn out? please send picture and/or video unless it blew up the camera ☺

Nothing.

ME: i hope the kids at ur school are getting nicer.

ME: the ones here r not.

ME: oh, and give me an update on
CODE NAME: WINTER BREAK? any progress??

Ever since Jude and I became friends in second grade, we've always had some sort of new mission we're working on. Usually they are secret missions that only the two of us know about, and they all start with "Code Name." Our current mission is to get our parents to let Jude come stay with me for a whole week over winter break.

ME: i really wish you were here right now.
i need my biffle ☹

*Biffle* means "BFFL," which means "best friend for life," which is exactly what Jude and I are. We like spelling it out because it's a silly word, like *sniffle* or *whiffle*.

Jude must be busy. Maybe her family is starting their own Sunday-morning tradition. I lean back in my chair and look out my bedroom window, trying to ignore the cannonball of disappointment settling in my stomach. I really need Jude right now.

The window on one wall faces the street, and the other window looks out onto the backyard. I love the back window because it's in the shape of a circle, and because my bedroom is on the second floor I can see far off into the distance. We have a fence all the way around our yard, but then past our yard is just woods, as far as I can see. It's always reminded me of an enchanted forest, like the kinds that you see in movies or read about in stories.

I try to think about that: the enchanted forest just on the other side of my backyard—instead of worrying about what's really going on with Gramps.

No one in my family ever tells me anything. Everyone thinks I'm too young—a *toddler*, like Noah says—but I'm not. They think all I do is daydream about dragons and fairies and outer space, but the truth is I have a lot of things on my mind. It just makes me feel better to have my head in the clouds sometimes. But with Jude gone and Noah's buttheadedness, and now that Gramps might be losing his mind or something, can anyone really blame me? The clouds are a lot more fun.

I glance back to my screen to see if Jude responded, but she hasn't.

Sighing, I pull my sketchbook from my bedside table where I left it last night when I was drawing before bed. I thumb through the pages, the chronicles of S. Hawkins, intergalactic teenage time traveler, trying to find her best friend and partner, who is trapped in an alternate time-line in the Andromeda Galaxy.

Usually, working on my graphic novel lets me forget

all the things that are not going right, like with Jude, and now Gramps. Last night I left off just as S. Hawkins wakes up on her spaceship, which has crash-landed on the planet Earth.

My pencil scratches against the paper fast, sketching the outline of her space suit as she stumbles out of the smoking aircraft in the middle of a field in a land called "UTAH," her malfunctioning GPS tells her right before it goes haywire. She looks all around, taking samples of the vegetation to bring to her home planet—text bubble: *IF SHE CAN MAKE IT BACK THERE*.

Next panel: S. Hawkins sees a forest of tall trees, a rocky mountain range in the distance, and she knows she'll have to make it over the mountains to find help. She walks toward the dense tree line, wondering if the first earthlings she meets will be friends or foes . . .

Just then, there's a howl in the woods.

I look up from my sketch, and I'm back in my room. I can't tell if I imagined the howl in my pages or if it really happened.

I check my laptop again. Still nothing from Jude.

Well, S. Hawkins helped for a little while, anyway.

Downstairs, Noah is sitting on the couch with a strand of red licorice hanging out of the side of his mouth, playing video games with the volume turned all the way up. I tell him I'm going outside, but I don't think he even hears me. Or else he's just gone back to ignoring me again.

I don't need a jacket because even though it's fall, it's a bright, sunny day. I try to think about what I would be doing right now if this were an ordinary day. Things still *seem* very ordinary:

There are birds pecking at feeders in the yard.

A squirrel runs along the telephone wire like a tight-rope walker.

A dog barks in the distance.

After breakfast, on a normal Sunday, I would usually go out to Mama's "She Shed" to help with her latest mosaic (which is a type of art). My job is to—very carefully, wearing goggles and gloves and all the other safety equipment—smash up old chipped dishes and glass and ceramic tiles into small pieces that Mama uses to make pictures. She uses glue and cement to put the pieces back together again like a puzzle, only you're not sure what the puzzle is supposed to look like until she's done.

I cup my hands around my eyes and look inside the window of the She Shed and see all of Mama's supplies neatly put away in boxes. The mosaic we were working on is only half-finished, propped against the wall. I realize the last time we were actually out in the She Shed was weeks ago. We haven't been out back in ages.

I walk down the stone path that leads out to the fairy fortress that lines the base of the biggest tree in the backyard, the one that has a hollowed-out kid-sized hole that Jude and I used to pretend was a portal to the enchanted part of the forest. That's why we chose that tree to build our fairy fortress around in the first place. The fairy fortress started out as "Code Name: Pixie Dust," a mission to protect the magic fairy portal that lives inside the tree. Whenever Jude and I found special rocks or shells or other tiny things that were unique, we would add them to the fortress.

Or at least we used to, when she was still here.

Looking at it now, I see how dirty and dingy I've let it get. There isn't a trace of the rainbow glitter we used to sprinkle over the fortress grounds, and the polished stones and gems and pieces of discarded mosaic tile are all covered in a coat of dirt. The little ceramic unicorn figurine that we found at the dollar store has sunken sideways into the mud. I adjust its position and try to anchor it into the ground so that it is standing up straight again. I clear away some of the brown fall leaves and prop up a few of the pretty red and yellow ones. If there really are such things as fairies, they are probably not very happy with how I've been neglecting their fortress ever since Jude left.

Not that I still believe in fairies.

Maybe growing up is sort of like a mosaic too. Like putting together pieces of a puzzle, but the picture you're trying to make keeps changing.

I hear barking coming from the woods beyond our backyard. There are old paths and trails that run through the woods, and sometimes people in the neighborhood hike them, and sometimes they bring their dogs with them, so it's not that unusual. The part that is unusual is that the barking sounds like it's getting closer, louder, and more insistent.

I take a few steps away from the fairy fortress and begin walking toward the back fence to see if I can get a better look. I reach the gate that leads out into the woods, and the barking gets louder.

Underneath all the other sounds—the barking, the rustle of dried leaves under my feet, the swish of the wind around me—I hear something else: a word, a feeling.

*Help!*

Looking all around, I can't tell which direction it's coming from. I cup my hands around my mouth and call, "Hello?"

*Please help!*

It's like a voice in my head, but not my own. To the left, I see the leaves of the overgrown shrubbery moving and shaking. Even though I know Moms don't like me going into the woods by myself, I lift the latch of the gate.

*Can you hear me?*

I glance back toward the house. There's no time to get Noah; this is urgent.

The branches and brush tremble like there is an invisible wave moving through them. As I walk toward the bushes, everything suddenly gets very still and quiet. I squint, trying to see beneath the layers of leaves and branches. That's when I see two eyes, one blue and one brown, watching me closely.

It's a dog!

"Hey," I whisper. The dog stands still, like maybe it's just as surprised to see me. I take a step closer. "Are you friendly?"

*Are you?*

"Me?" I say out loud, looking around for the source of this voice. "Hello? Is anybody here?"

There are lots of reasons I shouldn't go any closer—I remember all the times my veterinarian mom has told me, "Just because an animal is cute doesn't mean it can't be dangerous." I know. I remember. It could have rabies or be aggressive or feral. But Mom isn't here; she can't see how sweet its eyes are. Those aren't rabies eyes. They aren't feral eyes. They're soft and kind and curious, and its stance is relaxed.

I kneel down on the ground, not speaking so my voice doesn't scare it, thinking really hard, *It's okay, doggy*. I hold my hand out to be sniffed, palm up like Mom says to do. *I won't hurt you.*

It blinks, and I swear I hear that voice in my head again say, *Okay, I believe you.*

I blink back, and slowly, the dog fully emerges from the cover of greenery, with its head—no, *her* head—low and her nose wiggling, her tail wagging slowly and evenly, calm as she sniffs the air between us.

*Come here*, I say in my head, stretching my fingers toward her.

She's not wearing a collar, so that makes me wonder if anyone is even looking for her. As she moves closer, I see that she is not like any dog I've ever seen before. Her coat is speckled in dots and spots of brown and red and tan and white and gray and every shade in between. I can feel her breath on my hand as she sniffs. Just like her two eyes are different from each other, so are her ears. One of them is pointy and the other is floppy.

Our eyes meet again, and I suddenly feel hungry and tired, just like she must be.

As she nuzzles the top of her head into the palm of my hand, I see that she has a small cut above her blue eye, and she limps a little with each step. The tiny hairs on my arms stand up, and somehow I can feel how very afraid she's been. But even if she is a little scared, she lets me run my hand along her flank and behind her ears until she sits down in front of me.

She starts licking at her front paw, seeming bothered by it. Every time she sets it on the ground, she lifts it back up right away.

Slowly, I hold my hand out and she lets me take her paw. I try to tell her again with my thoughts that it's okay. She lets my fingers feel around the bottom of her paw. I find something sharp and pointy stuck right between two of her paw pads. I grab it with my fingers and very slowly, very gently, pull on it.

She lets out a huge yelp and jumps away from me.

"I'm sorry," I tell her out loud. "But look, it's all gone now. Look," I say, holding out the prickly burr that had been stuck in her paw. She steps toward me again, no longer limping. Cautiously, she picks up the burr between her teeth and shakes it back and forth like she wants to make sure it's really dead and gone and won't hurt her again.

"There," I say. "See?"

I start thinking about the leftovers in the refrigerator that might be a snack fit for a dog, my brain also checking off the list of poisonous ingredients on the poster at Mom's vet clinic: onion, garlic, grapes, chocolate. But I could probably feed her some string cheese or baby carrots, maybe some animal crackers would be okay. Cat food might even work. She licks her mouth almost like she can read my mind.

"Are you hungry, girl?"

Her right ear perks up and her big bushy foxtail wags back and forth just once. I look into the woods to make sure no one is coming for her, and then I stand, determined to get her to follow me into the yard so I can feed her. She backs away at first, but I pat my hand against my leg and she starts to follow me.

I walk slowly so the dog doesn't get spooked. I wish Mom were home right now so she could look at the dog right away to see if she's really okay or not. When I glance behind me, the dog has stopped and is standing still. Her right ear is on alert again, like she hears something that I don't. Just then, I hear the familiar screech of the back door opening, and when I look toward the house, I see Noah standing on the back porch.

"Sadie! Where are you?"

Before I can even turn back to the dog, I hear her feet scrambling against the ground to run away into the woods.

"Wait! It's okay. Come back, girl. It's okay," I say one more time, but she's already so far away I can't even tell which direction she went. Noah calls my name again.

"Noah, shut up!" I yell back.

By the time I make it back to the yard Noah has started walking toward the open gate. He says, "You're in so much trouble if I tell Moms you were wandering off into the woods."

"I wasn't *wandering*," I correct. "There was a dog."

He looks into the woods and then says, "Where?"

"She's gone now! You scared her with your yelling, and she ran away!"

"You shouldn't be messing with a dog you don't know."

I knew that was true—this was one of the very first lessons I ever remember learning in my life—but the thing was, it felt like I actually did know this dog somehow.

I go back inside with Noah, but when he puts his headset on and starts talking to whoever he is playing against on his video game, I know he won't bother to check on me again for a while.

In the kitchen I quietly open the cabinet, sneaking out a can of Catniss's food. The grinding sound of the can opener makes her come running. I turn the can upside down onto a plate, and the blob of can-shaped Ocean-fish Delight fills the kitchen with a terrible fish-tank stink. Catniss starts meowing so loud I'm scared she is going to give me away, so I drop a spoonful of the mush into her bowl and whisper, "Shhh, this isn't for you."

Next, I fill a big bowl with water and, along with the plate of cat food, bring it out to the clearing where the dog came out of the woods. I call and whistle and watch and wait for what seems like forever. But she doesn't come back.

## Chapter 3

# RESPONSIBILITY

All day long I keep my eyes on the backyard from the round window in my bedroom. I use my bird-watching binoculars to try to see deeper into the woods, just in case I can spot the dog somewhere out there. I take breaks to check my laptop, but Jude still hasn't responded.

*Come back*, I think, throwing my thoughts to her as hard as I can.

At my desk, I take out my box of 132 colored pencils, which I received for my tenth birthday, and flip to a new page in my *S. Hawkins* sketchbook. Sometimes when I'm drawing, I feel like I'm in another place, almost like a dream, and time can pass all around me without me even knowing it.

Text bubble: *The first earthling S. Hawkins meets is a furry creature like none she's encountered before in all of her travels, but who is lost just like she is . . .*

I always start with the eyes, whether they belong to a

person, an alien, or even a dog. Gramps taught me that trick—he knows all about drawing because he used to draw political cartoons for the newspapers. He showed me a bunch that he had saved, and even though the colors had faded and I didn't understand what most of them were about, I could still tell they were amazing.

For her left eye, I choose Slate Blue, blending it with Cream White and just a hint of Metallic Silver. For the right eye, I use a combination of Burnt Ochre, Sienna Brown, and Dark Umber. From there, I go on to draw the outline of her head, with her one floppy ear and one pointy ear. I continue to outline her body, making sure to get her fluffy foxtail just right. I start gathering the colors I need to make all the shades of her fur; I'm pretty sure I'll need to use about ninety-nine different pencils to get it right.

Suddenly I hear Noah calling from downstairs, "Moms are home!"

I look down at my drawing and it's nearly finished. Her fur has all the different colors blended together. And I drew the trees and woods all around her—I don't even remember doing that. Outside, the light has changed and I can tell it must be nearly dinnertime.

"And Gramps is with them," Noah yells again.

I race down the stairs, prepared to greet Gramps and tell Moms about the dog and to ask if we can make our special French toast breakfast for dinner—I love breakfast-for-dinner nights—but when I step into the kitchen I feel like I'm walking into a wall.

Not an actual wall, an invisible one made up of emotions and tension and people being upset. It's the kind of wall that stops me in my tracks.

Gramps is standing in the middle of the living room, tightly holding on to the handle of a briefcase, like if he lets it go, he might float away. There are two more big pieces of luggage sitting in the entryway.

"Noah?" Mom calls, as she hangs up her coat in the closet by the front door. "Will you come help put Grandpa's bags in the guest bedroom?"

"Hey, Gramps," Noah says as he walks across the room toward the two suitcases. But Gramps doesn't say anything; he just keeps holding on to that briefcase, looking very different than usual. I wonder if he got a haircut or if it's how his jacket is zipped all the way up to his chin. But then I realize why he looks so strange: He's not smiling. I don't think I've ever seen Gramps when he hasn't been smiling.

Mom walks into the living room and flips the switch on the wall, and as the big overhead light turns on, Gramps blinks and it looks like he has just woken up, sort of like when I've been drawing and suddenly realize that time has passed. He looks around the room, and that's when I notice something else: he has a big Band-Aid on his forehead, and I wonder what happened.

I wave at him, and slowly, he raises his arm to wave back. Finally, he sets his briefcase down on the floor next to him, and I wonder if he can feel the stickiness of the air like I can. He's moving like he does, anyway.

Mom walks up to Gramps and says, "Dad, do you want to sit?" Mom offers her arm to Gramps, but he doesn't take it. Instead, he looks at her with his sad, frowning eyes, making his face seem older and unfamiliar.

"I'm perfectly capable of walking," he snaps at her. That's not like him either, to talk to Mom, or anyone, in that way. Gramps walks off down the hall that leads to the guest bedroom, and Mom stands there in the middle of the living room next to Gramps's briefcase, looking at the floor.

Mama comes in through the door then, breaking up all that gooey, sticky tension in the room. She's carrying two square cardboard boxes stacked one on top of the other, and says, "We come bearing pizza!"

"Yes!" Noah shouts as he skip-walks back into the living room. "I'm starving!"

Taking the boxes from Mama's hands, Noah brings them to the kitchen where I'm still standing. And suddenly I can move again, those invisible walls having dissolved.

"Sadie, will you get out some plates, please?" Mama asks, giving my shoulder a squeeze as she walks past me.

"Sure," I say. I know that this is not the time to mention how I wanted to make French toast for dinner.

"Thanks," she says quietly, adding, more to herself than to anyone else, "It's been a *long* day."

Mom walks over to the kitchen where we're all standing and lets out a sigh as she sits down at the table. Her mascara is smudged under her eyes, but she smiles anyway and asks, "So did you two get along today?"

I think Noah will tattle on how I left the yard to go into the woods, but he just shrugs, takes a bite of pizza, and mumbles, "I guess."

We sit down to eat our slices, and I ask, "Should we wait for Gramps?"

Mom shakes her head. "I don't think Gramps is in the mood for pizza. He probably just needs some quiet time. We'll see if he's hungry later."

Noah has already eaten three slices of pepperoni, and Mama and I each have one from the veggie pizza. Mom has a slice of each, but she's not eating either one. She's just staring off into space. No one is talking. Not even Noah, and he's always saying something.

"I found a dog today," I end up saying, just so it's not so quiet. "I think it's lost, because it didn't have a collar—*she* didn't have a collar, I mean. It was a girl dog."

Noah kicks my foot under the table.

"A dog?" Mama says. "Where was she?"

Noah raises his eyebrows and looks at me with wide eyes: a warning.

"She was in the woods," I say, ignoring Noah and his *eyebrows*.

Mama looks at Noah now like he's in trouble, but I don't understand why anyone has to be in trouble at all. Nothing bad happened, except for the part where the dog ran back into the woods.

Noah holds his hands up in front of him and says, "Hey, she snuck out!"

"Sadie, you know you're not supposed to go into the woods by yourself," Mama scolds. "And I know we taught you better than to approach any dog you don't know."

"But she was calling me."

Noah mumbles through a mouthful of pizza, "You're such a weirdo."

"Noah," Mama says, giving him a *look*. Then to me, she says, "I'm sure she belongs to someone, Sadie. She probably just wandered off the trail."

"But she was limping, and she had this cut above her eye," I tell her, pointing to my own eyebrow. "Mom, I thought maybe you and me could go and look for her after dinner?"

I wait, but when she doesn't respond I repeat, "Mom?"

"Honey?" Mama places her hand on Mom's arm.

"Oh," she says, blinking her eyes like she's just woken

up from a daydream, the way Gramps had earlier. "Sorry, what?" she says, looking around the table.

"Mom, I was telling you about the dog I found today."

She looks down at her plate, where she hasn't touched her pizza, and says, "I'm sorry, I guess I wasn't paying attention." She pauses, frowning. "I think I might go upstairs and take a little nap. I'm feeling pretty tired."

"But Mom, what about the dog? I think she needs—"

"We'll talk about the dog later, okay?" Mom says as she starts to stand up from the table.

"But Mom—" I try again.

This time Noah interrupts me. "*But Mo-om*," he mimics me as he shoves half a slice of pizza in his mouth.

Butthead.

"I'll be up in a bit," Mama tells Mom as she leaves the room. Mama waits until we hear Mom's footsteps on the stairs before she sits down on the edge of the seat next to me, and says, "Listen, Grandpa is coming to live with us and it's going to be a big adjustment for everyone. I'm going to need you all to take on more responsibility. You are old enough to understand this," she says. "And Noah, this goes for you too."

"What did *I* do?" he says.

This time *I* shoot Noah a look.

"There are going to be some changes happening around

here, and it's important that we all understand what those changes are," she continues.

"Changes about Gramps?" I ask.

"Yes, about Gramps," she answers. "But also about all of us."

"What happened to his head?" Noah asks.

"Well," Mama begins, looking back and forth between the two of us. "Grandpa had a little fall in the middle of the night, and he bumped his head."

"Is he . . ." I stop, because I don't know what to say. "Okay?" I finish.

"Yes, he's okay, but he needs a little bit more help with things," she explains.

I feel tiny stings in the corners of my eyes when she says that, but I don't want to cry. Especially not in front of Noah because then that will just prove to him that I really am a baby.

"My love, it's okay," Mama says to me, rubbing my back in a soft circle. "The older people get, the easier it is to get hurt. Sometimes they don't see as well or move around as well anymore. It's just a part of people growing older."

I nod, and blink back the tears in my eyes.

"Mama, is Gramps . . ." I switch to a whisper before finishing. "Losing his mind?"

She starts, but then pauses, squinting like she's deciding

how much she should tell me. "Sadie, I don't want us to think of it in that way. Gramps has just been getting a little bit confused every once in a while. And it's our job to help him to feel at home here with us. Like all those times he used to watch you two and take care of you when you were younger. Now it's our turn to help take care of him."

"For how long?" Noah asks. "It's not like he's going to get better, right?"

Mama and Noah share a look, as if there's more to this than they're telling me. Then Mama finally answers, "It's hard to say right now. Why don't we all look at this as a sort of trial period; we'll just see how things go with Gramps being here."

I have so many questions, like what exactly does he need to get better *from*, and what happens *after* this trial period, and what if things *don't* go well, then what? But thinking about the possible answers sends my stomach into knots. So instead, I ask, "Can we still do fun things together, though?"

"Of course. He is still your Grandpa, and he still loves you just the same as he always has—both of you."

I look in the direction of Gramps's room down the hall, and I really hope that is true.

## Chapter 4

# ANIMAL CRACKER TRAIL

Later that night, after Mom and Mama say their good-nights and the house is quiet, I'm wide-awake. I turn over to one side, then the other. I fluff my pillow, but I can't get comfortable. I squeeze my eyes shut, but I can't stop picturing the way Gramps looked earlier.

*I'm here!*

I sit up and throw my covers off, listening closer.

That voice again. The dog.

I'm torn. I want to be responsible, like Mama said. I know it's important to not cause any extra stress right now, but helping a lost dog is important too.

There's a bark outside.

I am careful to be as quiet as possible as I grab the flashlight I always keep on my bedside table and tiptoe down the stairs. I sneak out through the back door with the flashlight, a box of animal crackers, and the travel bottle I always bring to school for water.

I turn on the flashlight and shine it on the ground in front of me, along the stone path, past the fairy tree and the She Shed, and down to the gate at the edge of the woods. I unlatch the gate like I did earlier. I shine the light ahead of me, and I can tell before I even get there that the cat food is gone. The plate is licked clean, and the big bowl of water is nearly empty too.

I refill the bowl with the water from my bottle and shake out a generous serving of animal crackers onto the empty plate.

I wait for a few minutes. But there's no sign of her.

Not wanting to be gone from my bed for too long, I leave the gate unlatched, just in case she might be able to use her nose to follow my scent to the house. Quickly and quietly, I sprinkle a trail of animal crackers behind me, leading from the spot where she came out of the woods all the way through the yard and up to our back door. I turn off the flashlight, and as I open the screen door that leads into the kitchen, I jump when I see Gramps standing there at the counter, holding a butter knife.

"What on earth are you doing?" Gramps whispers, and that's when I realize he is making himself a peanut butter and jelly sandwich.

"Oh, um . . . I—um—I'm leaving these snacks for . . . the fairies." I stutter.

"*Sassafras*," he says, more firmly. "I may be old, but I can still tell when you're full of applesauce."

As he sits at the table with his sandwich, he asks, "Want half?"

I sit down next to him and nod, because he really does make the world's best PB&J sandwiches. He places half of his sandwich on a paper towel and slides it in front of me.

"Do you want some animal crackers?" I ask, tilting the open end of the box in his direction. He nods and takes the box from me, the animal crackers making *tink tink tink* sounds in the quietness as they fall onto his plate.

I can't stop staring at the bandage on his forehead.

"What's on your mind?" he asks, like he can sense all the questions swirling around my head.

The thing is, for the first time in my life I don't know what to say to Gramps. Because all I want to ask him is about what happened at his apartment the night before, if he's really okay. But I don't want him to worry about me being worried, so instead I say, "Can you keep a secret?"

"Better than most," he answers, bringing a lion to his mouth. "Shoot."

"Well, there's this dog." I begin, and tell him the whole story, including all the details about her fur and her two different-colored eyes, because Gramps always likes to hear the details of a story. "And I was trying to get her to come back to the yard . . ."

"With a breadcrumb trail," he finishes. "Well, animal cracker trail, in this case."

"Exactly," I say. "I was trying to get Mom to help me look for her, but she just wasn't listening."

"I know the feeling, kiddo," he says, shaking his head. "I know the feeling."

We sit like that while each of us finishes our half of the sandwich, and I start to think that maybe Gramps isn't losing his mind after all. He's not acting any differently right now. Maybe it's that no one is listening to him either.

Just then, the kitchen light turns on and Mom is standing there in her pajamas. She crosses her arms when she sees us. "What's going on in here?" she asks. "It's almost midnight."

Gramps looks at the time on the stove and says, "Yes, it is. That's why it's called a *midnight* snack."

"Midnight snack, huh?" Mom says, giving a little grin. "Well, tomorrow is a school day, and we want to start the week off right, don't we, Sadie?"

I shrug. "I wasn't tired."

Mom continues, "Come on, you know you've got to get a good night's sleep or you'll wake up late and not want to go to school in the morning, and—"

"Come on, Katie, it's just a case of the Mondays." Gramps waves his hand in my direction. "Let the kid finish her sandwich."

Mom gives Gramps a look she usually reserves for Noah or me when we're being difficult. "Dad, it's a little more serious than"—she hooks her fingers into air quotes—"'the Mondays.' Remember I told you about Sadie needing an IEP this year?"

"A *who*?" Gramps says.

"Individualized. Education. Plan," Mom says, separating each word. "For her learning disability."

I feel my stomach tighten and twist.

Gramps shrugs. "First I've heard of it, Katie."

"Well, it's not the first time I've told you, but all right," she mutters, getting frustrated with him. "It's to help with her focus and attention issues."

"*Mom*," I groan. It bothers me how my moms just freely talk about this whole LD thing like I'm not even here.

"What?" she says. "It's not a secret, and there's nothing to feel embarrassed about. Everybody learns differently— tons of students have IEPs, Sadie."

"I know, but—" *But I don't want to be different.* Except I don't say that. Instead, I change the subject. "Wait, Gramps. What's the Mondays?"

"You don't know about the Mondays? Well," Gramps

begins, a smirk suddenly tugging at the corners of his mouth. "The Mondays is a mysterious illness of stomachaches and headaches and coughs and imaginary fevers and bad dreams, and all kinds of other symptoms that your mother used to get when she was around your age. It would come on just when the school week was about to start," he says, snapping his fingers. "Like clockwork."

"Okay, Dad," Mom sighs, sitting down at the table. Then to me, "Sadie, off to bed now. And make sure you brush your teeth again now that you've had your midnight snack."

I slink out of the chair and I say my goodnights, leaving Mom and Gramps in the kitchen.


**The next morning** when my alarm goes off, I don't hit snooze, even though I really want to. But that would mean Mom was right about me not getting enough sleep. So I get out of bed and go downstairs in my frog slippers.

Moms are already sitting at the kitchen table, each with their morning cup of coffee. A selection of cereal boxes is on the table, with bowls and milk and toast and orange slices.

"Look who's up already," Mama says, and then gives me a wink only I can see.

"Nice surprise," Mom adds, and she seems much more

like herself today. "We were just about to flip a coin to see which one of us was going to try to wake you up."

I walk over to the door and see that the trail of animal crackers is gone.

"Hey, did you see that dog I was telling you about?" I ask.

"No," Mama says, looking out the window. "But don't worry; I'm sure someone will find her."

"I don't think anyone's looking, though," I say.

"You don't know that," Mom says.

"But she didn't have a collar," I tell them again. "Besides, I just have a feeling that we're supposed to be looking for her."

Mom gives Mama one of her *looks*, one that says she's not really taking me seriously, and says, "Tell you what, I will check with the shelter when I get in today and ask around to see if anyone knows anything about a missing dog in the woods. How 'bout that?"

"Okay," I say. "I drew a picture of her, if you want to take it with you to show people."

I start to get up to go get the drawing from my bedroom, and Mom stops me. "Wait, let's just finish your breakfast first and get ready for school, and then we can worry about the drawing. One thing at a time, right?" she reminds me.

"All right," I say, but as I look down at my slowly

soggifying cereal I feel a shadowy blob fall over the kitchen. "*Ughh*," I groan, rubbing my stomach. Just thinking about school is making my stomach start to hurt for real. "I really don't feel good."

Just then, Noah comes into the kitchen, already dressed for school, and sets his backpack on the floor next to his chair at the table. Sitting down in the seat opposite me, he cups his hands around his mouth and whispers—loud enough for only me to hear—"Faker!"

"Am not," I mutter, and Moms look at me like I'm the one trying to start an argument.

Noah doesn't understand. School has always been easy for him. He never had to have an IEP. He's good at everything and has tons of friends—although I don't know why.

Noah scrunches up his face and sticks out his tongue when Moms aren't looking, and then stuffs a slice of toast into his mouth, mumbling, "Better get ready. If you're late for school again, you'll get . . . *dun, dun, dun*," he says in a creepy, scary-movie voice, "detention!"

"Noah, enough," Mama says. "You're not helping." Then to me, she adds, "I'm sorry you're not feeling good, I am. But we've talked about this."

Mom continues, picking up the conversation we've had so many times. "You know that once you get dressed and get your things organized and are on your way it won't be so overwhelming and you'll start feeling better."

"I know," I say, not wanting to get into the whole thing all over again. I leave the table to start getting ready, but not before sticking my tongue out at Noah on my way out.

## Chapter 5

# THE BUS STOP

It's weird, ever since I found out about my processing disorder—which is what my LD is—Moms have acted like it all makes so much sense: why I've never gotten good grades and why I've always hated school so much, why I can understand something when Mama (who teaches high school) helps me study at home and then fail a test on it the next day.

Knowing that I actually have something—a disorder, or as my moms always say, *a difference*—has only made me dread school more than ever. Because now I have to go to the Resource Room after lunch every Tuesday and Thursday. When everyone else is in class getting free time, I have to complete *extra* lessons in math—which doesn't seem fair. I can't help but feel like I'm being punished.

But that's not why I take my time getting to the bus stop every day. I always try to time my arrival so I don't have to stand there with the other kids from my school. The bus stop is this weird in-between space that's not home and not school. Without parents or teachers, it's like there are no rules about how you're supposed to act—or, at least, people pretend there aren't.

Today, I pace myself, whistling into the woods on my way, calling for the dog. I stop every so often to peer between the trees with my bird-watching binoculars, but I don't see any sign of her.

I blame the bus for the carnival of suckage that fifth grade has become. It started on the very first day of the year, before school even started, before I got my IEP and had to start going to the Resource Room.

After all, it was on the bus that first morning of the year when I became the archenemy of the meanest kid at school. Her name is Macy, also known as "Mean Machine" for two reasons: The first is that her last name is MacHine, which looks like "machine," even though it's not pronounced that way. The second reason is because everyone remembers how last year, she got into *two different fights* with kids who were older than us. Macy is always glaring at everyone, like she's looking for the poor sorry soul who will become her next victim.

Unfortunately, this year, that poor sorry soul is me.

It was an accident. On the first day of school, I stepped on the back of Macy's sneaker as we were walking onto the bus. Which wouldn't have been that bad, except that when I stepped on her shoe it came right off. Which also wouldn't have been that bad, if she hadn't tripped and fallen down in front of everyone on the bus. I thought she might scream or push me or even punch me, but she turned around and growled at me. *Growled.* Somehow, that felt worse.

Everyone whooped and hollered and said that Macy was going to kill me. They thought I did it on purpose to make fun of her, but I would never do something like that. I told Macy I was sorry and I asked if she was okay and I tried to explain what happened, but she wouldn't listen. I only stepped on her shoe because I had my *S. Hawkins* sketchbook open, drawing *while* I was walking, which was probably not the best idea.

As if that wasn't bad enough, another kid from my class, Bailey, snatched my book and started reading the *S. Hawkins* graphic novel *out loud* and passing it around to the entire bus, but when I tried to explain that it was not about an astronaut, but a time-traveling superhero *from* outer space, they just thought that was stupid. Or thought *I* was stupid. Either way, that is what led to the creation of my own nickname: Sadie "Spacegirl" Mitchell-Rosen.

I don't bring *S. Hawkins* to school anymore.

And I don't say anything as I approach the other kids at the bus stop—I never do. But that doesn't keep them from talking to me.

"Did you get dressed in the dark, Spacegirl?" It's Jayden, another kid in my grade, trying to look cool in front of the sixth graders by making fun of me.

"*No,*" I respond with as much attitude as I can muster. But then I follow where they're pointing, and I look down at my feet. My socks don't match: one is white and the other is blue with tiny orange goldfish swimming around and blowing bubbles.

Great.

Bailey cuts her eyes to me and snorts a quick chuckle in my direction. Moments like this, I wish Noah was still at my school. He may make fun of me all the time at home, but he'll always stick up for me if anyone else tries it.

I look at Macy's socks: they are both purple.

She glances over at the binoculars hanging around my neck.

"They're for bird-watching," I explain.

"I don't care," Macy mumbles, and shrugs in return. I think those are the most words I've ever heard Macy say, to me or to anyone, for that matter.

"I mean, I wasn't bird-watching just now. I was looking for a lost . . . dog . . ." I trail off because Macy has already turned away from me. I'm not sure why I keep speaking; maybe just so the last thing said isn't Jayden's comment about my socks.

"You lost your dog?"

When I look up Macy's facing me, waiting for a response.

"Well, sorta. She's not exactly *my* dog," I begin. "But yeah, she's lost. Have *you* seen a dog around? She has two different-colored eyes and one floppy ear and one pointy ear and a big bushy tail."

Macy doesn't answer; she just shakes her head.

"Do you have one?" I ask her. "A dog, I mean."

She shakes her head again.

"I have a cat—well, she's technically my brother's cat, but . . ." I don't want to jinx it by talking anymore, so I stop mid-sentence.

"I have a rabbit," she offers.

"Oh."

I don't know what to say, so we don't say anything else as we wait for the bus to get there, and as we climb up the steps and walk down the aisle, I stay a few extra paces behind Macy so I never again step on the back of her shoe. Thankfully, there's an empty seat toward the middle—the middle is always the safest. You can get lost in the middle, not so much of a target.

The bus slogs down the road, and as it picks up speed I swear I see a flash of fur and a big bushy tail running through the trees alongside us.

*Wait! Wait for me!* I hear in my mind.

**During school, I** can't pay attention, but today it has nothing to do with my IEP or LD stuff. It's more that I can't get the dog out of my head. I keep checking the big clock on the wall, but it feels like time is moving extra slowly today.

I look over at Macy in the desk across the aisle from mine. She doesn't look like she's paying attention either—she is folding a piece of paper into a tiny bird; the inside of her desk is lined with a whole zoo of origami animals. Still, she somehow always gets perfect scores on her tests. She gets stickers and notes like "GREAT JOB!"

I only know because I see when she gets them back from Ms. Avery, which makes me wonder if she sees my grades when I get horrible scores, and notes like "SEE ME" written in big letters across the top.

I remember last year in fourth grade, when we were learning about Asian and Pacific Islander history, we had some guest speakers come to visit our class. And I remember one of the people who came was Macy's grandmother. She told us about what it was like growing up in Japan as a little girl. I liked her. She seemed *so* much nicer and friendlier than Macy, I wondered if they could really be related. But I could see the resemblance in their faces, even if Macy didn't smile nearly as much as her grandma. Macy has a sprinkling of freckles dusted over her nose and cheeks, and curly hair, sort of like mine—not straight and shiny like her grandmother's.

That day, Macy's grandma taught us some Japanese words (the only one I remember is *arigato*—"thank you"), and we also made candy sushi out of Rice Krispies Treats rolled up with gummy-fish filling and then wrapped with a green Fruit Roll-Up around the outside, like seaweed.

She also taught us step-by-step how to make an origami star, but I sucked at it because my fingers were all sticky from the candy sushi; my folds were all messy and uneven.

"Shhhh!" Bailey—the same Bailey from the bus stop— hisses, turning around in her seat to stare at me. "That's so annoying."

Only then do I realize that I've been tapping my pen against my desk, over and over again. "Oh," I whisper. "Sorry."

I glance to my side, and Macy is looking at me too, only this time she isn't glaring. I hold the pen still in my hand, but there are a series of blue dots speckled where I've tapped it against my desk. I lick my thumb and try to wipe the ink, but it only leaves behind a big smudge in the center of all the dots.

And right before my eyes, I start to see something take shape in between the dots and the smudge mark. The smudge is in the shape of something familiar. Like an animal. Like a . . . *dog*. And the dots: there are two of them right where her eyes would be. Ms. Avery's voice starts to fade away into the background of my mind. And the words on the whiteboard at the front of the room begin to look all squiggly and far away.

Next, the pen is moving, drawing trees and the two lines that form the road by the bus stop, and two blobs of varying heights stand on the side of the road. I squint to see them better, and as they come into focus, I realize those blobs are me and Macy, and the closer I look, the more detailed those blobs of us become. Like an animation, the dog seems to be running through the trees toward us. But she can't catch up, and she seems scared, like she's no longer running toward me, but away from something else. As she runs, she gets bigger and bigger, closer and closer.

Someone screams.

I fall out of my chair onto the floor. And then I realize the scream has come from my own mouth! As I look around, every single student in my class is staring.

"Sadie Mitchell-Rosen!" Ms. Avery shouts, marching up the aisle toward me. "Back in your seat right this instant!"

I scramble to my feet, taking too long to understand what has just happened.

"S-sorry, I—I—" I try to explain, but as I look down at my desk, I can feel my face turning hot and embarrassed.

"Did you do that?" Ms. Avery yells, pointing at the desk.

"I—I don't know," I reply, confused by what I am seeing.

Some of the kids whisper and snicker, and then Bailey turns around again with this crooked, mischievous smirk like a dash across her face, and says, "Sadie was scribbling all over the desk. I saw her do it."

I don't remember doing that, but as I look down, sure enough, there are blue pen marks all over the desk—lines and circles, more dots, the two blobs, and a circle around the smudge mark that spiraled bigger and bigger and bigger, like the dog running toward us, about to jump right off the desk.

"Principal's office," Ms. Avery says.

"But I didn't mean to—"

"Now!" Ms. Avery interrupts. I hang my head and start walking toward the door, when Ms. Avery calls out after me and says, "Wait—take your books and your backpack with you. We will find a later time for you to clean up the mess you made; you've disrupted the class enough for one day."

## Chapter 6

# DOODIE DUTY

Mom picks me up from school, and she is *mad*. This is the third time this school year that Mom has to come get me. The first two times were because I went to the nurse's office and pretended to be sick so I could leave school early—which, combined with my terrible grades last year, was one of the things that led to my moms having me tested for an LD in the first place.

Mom is quiet as we walk across the school parking lot toward her car. It isn't until we've left the school and are driving that she finally speaks.

"Do you want to tell me what happened?"

"I'm not even sure, Mom," I begin. "It wasn't my fault; it was like I was under a spell or someth—"

"No stories," Mom says, cutting me off. "Just tell me what actually happened."

"I fell asleep at my desk, and I was dreaming of the lost

dog I told you about. And it was like a movie playing in my mind. The dog was getting chased. I didn't know I was drawing on the desk either, Mom. I swear. Not until I fell out of my chair onto the floor."

Mom breathes in deeply and then lets out a long sigh. "What am I supposed to do with you?" She shakes her head and tightens her hands around the steering wheel.

"I didn't mean to—"

"Honey," she begins, but stops. "Let's just have some quiet time until we get to my work, all right?"

"Can't I stay home with Gramps?" I ask.

"No, you cannot," she says. "Grandpa needs his rest today."

It's like one of those invisible walls of gooey silence is rising up between us as Mom drives to the county animal shelter where she works. I can hear dogs barking from inside the building as she slows down and turns into the parking lot. Mom shuts the car off and unbuckles her seat belt.

"Honey, I need you to listen to me." She turns in her seat and reaches out to hold my hand. "Mama and I love your imagination; we love your stories and how creative you are. I don't want that to change. But when it comes to school, you've got to recognize when it's time for pretending and dreaming, and when it's time for real life and responsibilities."

"But Mom, this *was* real life!"

"Sadie, stop!" she raises her voice, but then pauses. "I don't know, maybe we need to set up another meeting to go over your IEP or—"

"No, Mom," I interrupt. "It's not that."

"Well"—she throws her hands up in the air—"then I don't know what else to say." She takes a deep breath, and continues, calmer, quieter. "It's not okay for you to get sent to the principal's office or stay home sick when things get tough or you're having a bad day at school. And you know I cannot keep leaving work in the middle of the day like this."

"I didn't mean to make you leave work, I promise," I try to tell her.

"Well, eleven years old is old enough to understand that actions have consequences."


**Consequences can mean** a lot of different things. Today, consequences mean *poop*. Actual poop.

"Doodie Duty," says Patrick, one of the vet techs. "That's what we call it around here: Doodie Duty!"

I follow Patrick into one of the back rooms of the animal shelter that is full of cages, from the floor to the ceiling. There's one room of crates that are just for cats, and one room of crates that are just for dogs. And they both stink.

It's our job to clean out every single cage.

"What did you do to get stuck with Doodie Duty?" I ask Patrick.

"Nothing." Then he asks me, "Why, what did *you* do?"

"Nothing," I lie at first, but then I say, "Okay, I got sent to the principal's office for drawing on my desk and falling out of my chair and disrupting the class. Mom had to come get me."

He laughs, and says, "Well, I might have been late to work a few too many days."

"I'm late a lot too," I tell him. "Mom doesn't like that."

"No, she doesn't," he agrees.

He hands me some gloves, a smock, a spray bottle, and a roll of paper towels, and we get to work cleaning the cages in the cat room. Mom stops in once before her next surgery to see how it's going, and she seems pretty happy with both Patrick and me. It goes by faster than I thought it would.

As we're about to start on the dog room, Patrick leaves to get more supplies. While I'm alone, I hear that voice again: *Hello?*

"It's just your imagination," I mumble to myself, attempting to ignore it. I try humming, scrubbing at a smudge on one of the crates. I don't need another reason for Mom to be mad at me.

*Are you there?*

I drop my paper towels and move toward the voice. It's coming from the kennel room. At first, I don't see anything strange. But then I hear a familiar bark coming from a separate room connected to the kennel. I hear the bark again, and again. I crack open the door to the room.

When I peek in, I can't believe what I see.

There is only one dog in a big crate against the wall.

I recognize her immediately.

"It's you!" I shout, and I walk over to her and kneel down, placing my hand against the bars for her to sniff me, so she knows who I am. She whines and licks the palm of my hand.

As I look into her two different-colored eyes, I hear a little voice in my head say, *You found me! I was calling you and you came!*

"I found you," I say out loud. I think back to how I saw her running through the woods from the bus window this morning.

*I was trying to catch up with you when they got me.*

I stand up and take a couple of steps backward. "There's no way I'm having a conversation with this dog," I say out loud.

*Dewey.*

"What?" I whisper.

*Dewey—that's my name.*

"Dewey?" I repeat, and the dog's ears perk up.

I wonder if Mom has been right about me this whole time and I really *don't* always know when it's time for pretending and time for real life. But as soon as I have that thought, I hear that small voice in my head say, *Thank you for the food; I was so hungry. And my paw feels so much better now.*

I must be losing my mind or something. I'm making this up. I have to be.

Dewey tilts her head to the side. *No, you're not.*

"Oh my gosh," I gasp, crouching back down in front of the crate again. "Are you . . . are you really talking to me somehow?"

*Yes, and we don't have a lot of time—I need you to get me out of here.*

"No, this isn't real," I tell the dog, shaking my head back and forth.

*Stop thinking that—and I told you, it's Dewey!* She barks twice, and that gets my attention. *Listen to me. I did something wrong, and now I'm in trouble. I only have until the end of the week. You have to get me out of here!*

"Why only until the end of the week?" I ask, adding uncertainly, "Dewey?"

I feel my hands moving to the latch on the door of the

crate. But just then, I hear Mom's voice yelling, "Sadie, no!" Mom pulls my arm away from the latch and gets in between the door and me. Dewey starts lunging and growling and barking, throwing her body against the bars, and all the while, I hear her voice screaming *no* in my head, like a howl but worse—sadder, lonelier, more desperate.

"But Mom," I begin. "This is her. This is the dog I was telling you about. She needs us."

"Sadie, you're not even supposed to be back here. What are you thinking? She could have attacked you!"

"She wouldn't—" *do that*, I was going to say, but Mom interrupts.

"I see you've been giving a lot of thought to what we talked about earlier," she snaps at me, with her hands on her hips, her voice sharp. "How actions have consequences."

"I *have* been thinking about that; I just—"

"Go get ready to leave." Mom points to the door, and when I look back at Dewey, she adds, "Right now!"

## Chapter 7

# IF ALL OF THIS IS REAL

We're having spaghetti with veggie meatballs for dinner tonight. Gramps makes a face as he takes his first bite. Normally that would crack me up, but my head is too full of other thoughts to find anything very funny right now.

"Sadie, you've been awfully quiet tonight," Mama says to me.

I shrug.

Mom replies, "That's probably because she's been doing some thinking about what happened today."

I *was* thinking about what happened today, but not in the way Mom means. She was talking about school and consequences, but I was thinking about what happened today at the shelter. I was thinking about Dewey.

"I can't believe you got kicked out—who gets kicked out of class in fifth grade?" Noah says.

Sometimes I really hate my brother.

I stab a veggie meatball with my fork and stuff it into

my mouth to stop myself from saying that out loud. Once I finish chewing and swallowing, I dab my napkin to the corner of my mouth, and then I say, in my most grown-up, responsible voice, "Moms, I want to ask you both a very serious question."

Mama sets her fork down and looks at me, and then Mom says, "Yes?"

"I want us to adopt a dog," I say. "I really feel very strongly about it, and I think a dog would make an amazing addition to our family. Plus, I know you both want me to be more responsible, and I have always wanted a dog. She—it—it would be my responsibility to feed and walk and play with every day. It would teach me responsibility."

"Yeah," Noah scoffs. "Every time I get kicked out of school, I ask for a new pet as a reward. Oh, wait," he says, then pauses. "I've never been kicked out of school before."

Sometimes I really, *really* hate my brother.

Mama looks at Mom, and then she says, "That's something we can think about, but we'll need to discuss it more."

I nod and continue, "Okay but the thing is, I already know which dog I want to adopt."

"No," Mom says immediately, setting her napkin on the table next to her plate. "Absolutely not."

"What?" Mama asks. "What's wrong?"

"If you seriously want to talk about getting a dog—" Mom begins, but I interrupt her.

"I don't want *a* dog. I want *that* dog."

"The answer is no, and that is final." She takes a sip of her drink, as if that marks the end of the conversation.

"But she only has until the end of the week to find a home!" I blurt out.

Mom sets down her glass and squints at me, "You were snooping in my files?" She says it like it's a question, but the sharpness of her tone tells me that she's not really asking; she's accusing.

"No," I try to say, but Mom just shakes her head like she doesn't believe me.

Mama looks back and forth between Mom and me. "What do you mean 'snooping'?"

"How else would you know that the dog is going to be euthanized at the end of the week?" Mom asks, crossing her arms.

Mama clucks her tongue. "Aw, that's too bad."

Euthanized. I know what that means.

It means death.

"That is, unless her owner claims her before then," I hear Mom continue in the background of my racing thoughts.

It means . . . that Dewey is right. And if Dewey is right, that means all of this is real, and if all of this is real, then we are actually communicating telepathically.

It means she really does need my help.

"But Moms, that is not fair," I argue, trying not to raise my voice.

"Sadie, that dog bit one of our handlers today. She is aggressive, reactive, and a huge bite risk," she says, counting the reasons on her fingers. "There are rules about biters; I don't make them, but I have to follow them."

"She was just scared," I yell. "She's a great dog."

"Sadie, there are two dozen *great* dogs at the shelter right now who are ready to be adopted." She shakes her head before continuing, "The point is: this dog is not adoptable."

"But—" I begin.

But Mom interrupts me. "You need to let it go, Sadie."

"Fine," I say, and I stomp up the stairs to my room.


**I can hear** them talking downstairs, underneath the clanging and clinking sounds of the dishes being collected and washed, while I get changed into my pajamas. I don't even believe what Mom said about Dewey. She was perfectly sweet to me. More than sweet, actually. She was practically . . . a *person*.

I check my laptop: nothing from Jude.

I tuck myself into bed and stare at the ceiling.

This dog is my friend already. And I don't have any other friends right now. At least not friends who are *here*, anyway. Why doesn't Mom care about that?

"Sassafras?"

I look over and see Gramps standing in my doorway. "Hi, Gramps."

"Just wanted to check on you." He walks over and sits down on the edge of my bed, smiling sadly, and says, "I'm sorry about the dog, my dear."

"The thing is, I know she's not a mean dog, but Mom doesn't care. She just doesn't want me to have any friends."

"Oh, that's applesauce and you know it," Gramps says, batting his hand at me. "I mean, I'm your friend, aren't I?" he says, pointing to himself.

"Yeah," I answer.

"So if your mom really didn't want you to have any friends, why would she have asked me to move in here?"

I think about it. "Okay," I say. "I guess you have a point."

"Lights out in ten minutes, everyone," Mom says in the hallway, and then she sticks her head into my room and says, "Did you brush your teeth?"

I cross my arms and don't answer.

"I don't *have* teeth," Gramps whispers to me after I don't say anything, tapping a fingernail against his shiny white dentures. "So she must be talking to you, kiddo."

Gramps stands to leave too, but I whisper, "Gramps, wait. Can I tell you something?"

He nods and says, "Anything."

"That dog is special," I say.

"I know she is," he agrees.

"No, I mean . . ." I pause. "I think she might be able to talk to me."

"Interesting." Gramps sits back down and says, "What did she sound like?"

"She wasn't really talking to me with words, but it was like I could hear what she was thinking in my head."

"I'd say that's a very special dog, indeed," he finally says.

"Do you—do you think I'm losing my mind?" I ask him. "Don't you think that's strange?"

He laughs and says, "The older I get, the more I think there are a whole lot of things in this world that we don't understand. So you think a dog is telepathically communicating with you? I've heard of stranger things."

"Really?" I ask, relieved.

"Really," he answers. "You catch some Zs tonight. I'm gonna go hit the hay too." He stands up and leans over to kiss my forehead.

"Good night, Gramps," I tell him.

He stops in my doorway, turns around, and says, "Sleep tight, Katie."

"Sadie," I correct.

"I know." He smiles. "That's what I said."

"Oh-kay," I say uncertainly.

## Part Two

# LOST AND FOUND

# Chapter 8

# ORIGAMI

Mama drives me to school a half hour early so she can meet with Ms. Avery. It's weird to walk through the halls when no one is here except for teachers. It's almost like a creepy dream, or an alternate universe that is a lot like my school but also a place I've never been before.

When we get to my classroom Ms. Avery hands me a plastic spray bottle filled with some kind of bluish-green cleaner, and a roll of brown paper towels, like the kind that are in the restroom, which for some reason my school calls a lavatory.

Jude and I used to make fun of the word because it sounded like *laboratory*. Anytime Jude had to go to the bathroom, she'd put on this weird mad-scientist kind of accent and say, "I have to go conduct an experiment!"

I start accidentally laughing out loud thinking about it now, but then I glance over at Mama and she shoots me a *look*.

*Sorry*, I mouth.

Mama and Ms. Avery leave the room to talk in the hall while I clean off my desk. I can see them standing out there through the little window in the door, but I can't be sure what they're saying.

I spray the top of my desk with the cleaner and watch as the pen marks of my drawing begin to flood and wave, getting all distorted and blurry. It makes me think about what Dewey said to me yesterday—how my weird dream-drawing was neither just a dream nor a drawing, but was what actually had happened to Dewey: she was trying to run to me, away from being caught, and that's exactly what I saw. As I wipe the spray with the paper towels, the drawing begins to slowly disappear. I spray again and make one more pass, and now the desk looks totally clean and shiny, except for a pointy-looking heart with an arrow through its center that someone carved into the top corner—probably years ago.

Mama comes in and tells me to "have a good day," but she raises her eyebrows all the way up her forehead and gives me another one of her *looks*, whispering so only I can hear, "Just remember all the techniques we've been going over when your mind starts wandering or you're having trouble staying focused."

"I know, Mama." Deep accordion breaths, in and out.

Count to seven. Name five things I can observe around me in the moment. We've been over this so many times.

After Mama leaves, it's just Ms. Avery and me in the room alone. She is drinking coffee at her desk, working on something. She doesn't say anything to me; sometimes I think she doesn't really believe I have an LD and she still just thinks I'm a lazy student, or worse, a troublemaker.

I look at the clock on the wall above the door; I still have ten minutes before anyone should be arriving, so I take my regular notebook out of my backpack. I can't be distracted if I'm not supposed to be doing anything in the first place.

I don't have my big box of colored pencils or my *S. Hawkins* sketchbook with me, but I do have my small set of nice drawing pencils Gramps gave me. I won't be able to capture all the shades of Dewey's fur, or her different-colored eyes, but I start to draw her anyway—the graphite makes smooth, creamy gray marks on the page.

I close my eyes and imagine opening the dog kennel at the shelter to let Dewey out. In my mind I can even see us playing together in the backyard, her walking on the trails with me, sleeping in my bed at night. I just know, somehow, that Dewey belongs with me—that I belong with her.

I draw out each scene in panels, just like I would draw

in my graphic novel. Except in the last drawing, I add a collar and a name tag in the shape of a bone. Inside the bone I write in my very best handwriting:

DEWEY

I hear some voices out in the hall, and that's when Ms. Avery stands up and goes to the classroom door. I hear her say good morning to someone, and I know I'll have to hurry up if I want to finish my drawings by the time class begins. Just then, the first of the students begin to enter the classroom—the walkers, I think. Once the bus riders are in, I'll have to stop. I keep my head down in my sketchbook and work fast to touch up my series of drawings.

Macy sits down in her regular seat next to mine, and I think—I *think*—she looks over and sort of smiles, just a tiny curve at the corner of her mouth. I lift my hand off my desk in an equally tiny wave.

Today we are watching a video about rovers exploring Mars, and ordinarily I would actually be interested, but Ms. Avery turns the lights off, which makes me feel instantly sleepy. I don't dare fall asleep again, though, because who knows what might happen *this* time.

The person narrating the film has a super-boring voice—I try to focus on their words. I take some deep breaths, in and out, like an accordion. But none of my techniques are helping today.

I glance around and see that Macy is busy creating another of her origami creatures, silently folding the paper over and over at different angles. I wonder if anyone is actually paying attention to the movie. When Macy looks at me, I quickly dart my eyes away in the direction of the screen.

But then I feel something tap the edge of my desk.

I pick the origami form up and examine the tight folds of valleys and edges—it's in the shape of a butterfly. I look up and smile at Macy, and mouth the words, *Cool, thanks.*

She shakes her head and mimes with her hands like she's unfolding, and she whispers, "Open."

I begin trying to figure out how to unfold the butterfly—it takes several different tries because it's so complicated—but finally the folds begin to open, and I can see that inside of the paper are words written in thin, swoopy letters:

*Hi, Sadie—*

*I just wanted to tell you I liked your drawing. I wish they would have let you keep your desk like that. It was a lot more interesting that way. I felt bad that you had to go to the office yesterday.*

*I personally think they should let us decorate our desks however we want. But I know they won't.*

*—m.m.m.*

I read her note a few times, amazed at how nice she's being to me. Under her words, I write back:

*Thank you! I also really like your ~~origomy origamy~~ (?) paper animals. I wish they would let us decorate our desks too. I ~~felt~~ feel like an idiot for falling out of my seat. Oh well, I guess*

*☺—Sadie*

I try to fold the note back up, but I have no idea where to start, so I just make a couple of folds and (careful not to let Ms. Avery see) reach across the aisle to set it on top of Macy's desk. I watch her unfold and read my note.

She writes something else and passes it to me again. Just then, the lights suddenly turn back on, and Ms. Avery moves to the front of the room and starts asking questions about the movie. I slide the paper onto my lap to read it.

In big letters under my note, she wrote:

*ORIGAMI . . . and thank you, I would like that too.*

Who would've guessed I actually have something in

common with Macy MacHine? Even if it is something as small as wishing we could decorate our desks.

I count down the minutes until lunchtime. Our class walks in a line toward the cafeteria, and even though we're supposed to be quiet because the third and fourth grade rooms that we pass are still in class, lots of the students are talking and laughing. If Jude were still here, I probably would be too, and we'd probably already have come up with a plan to save Dewey.

But she's not here.

I sit down in my usual spot at the middle of my classroom's lunch table, scrunched between two groups of friends, neither of which are mine, and begin unpacking my lunch bag: leftover pizza, a plastic container of animal crackers, and an apple. I take out my napkin, and I see a note written there in red pen:

*Have a good day! Love, Moms*

They never forget to leave me a note on my napkin. This might be one more thing that Noah would say makes me a baby, but I don't care—my napkin notes help me get through the school day.

I look down toward the end of the table, and I see Macy sitting with an open seat on either side. No one ever sits next to her. She has a paper animal sitting on the edge of her lunch tray. She always has at least one of her animals with her at lunch. Maybe it's sort of like my napkin note—her paper creatures are just one of the things that make the school day a little easier.

I collect my lunch items and put them back into my lunch bag, stuff my napkin note into my pocket, and stand up. I feel Bailey's laser eyes watching me relocate. When I get to the end of the table where Macy is sitting, I can see that today she has the origami bunny on her tray.

I stand by the seat next to her, clear my throat, and say, "Can I sit here?"

She lifts one shoulder and says, "I guess."

So I do. I don't say anything as I take out my sketchbook—I turn past the pages of Dewey drawings, and I try not to let her see as I begin a brand-new drawing of the origami bunny that is sitting out right in front of me. Quickly, I draw out the pointy lines that make up the rabbit's ears and face and body and tail in my sketchbook.

Macy nudges the paper bunny toward me, and when I look up, she says, "You can hold it, if you want. I mean, if it would help."

Carefully, I pluck the paper rabbit with two fingers and set it in the palm of my hand. I'm just about to start drawing when suddenly Bailey leans across the table and sneers, talking above everyone else in our class. "Oh look,

Mean Machine and Spacegirl finally found a friend—how sweet!" She coos, puckering her lips, "Too bad you're both losers."

I open my mouth, trying to find the perfect retort—the one that will shut Bailey up for good—but she has already gone back to her own conversation, not even thinking of me or Macy anymore. "Jerk," I mutter to myself.

At first, I think Macy didn't hear me because she doesn't say anything right away. But then she looks at me, the edges of her mouth twitching like she's trying not to smile. "You know what?" she says. "I wish I *was* a machine. Then I could figure out a way to reboot Bailey's personality."

Her words wrap around me like a warm blanket, and, for the first time since Jude left, I remember what it feels like to *belong* again.

"And I wish I had a spaceship," I reply, barely containing my chuckle. "I'd use it to send her to the moon."

"No, farther—send her to Mars!"

"Or maybe," I add, "she could just hang out in Saturn's rings for a while to think about what a jerk she is. A brand-new kind of detention!"

Macy covers her mouth and giggles, then goes back to eating her lunch.

As I hold the origami bunny in my hand, I realize it's

not really that fragile at all. It's stiff and sturdy. I can't figure out how Macy transformed what was once just a flat piece of paper into this creature that looks like it could hop right out of my hand.

It's nearing the end of the lunch period by the time I look up to find that Macy has been watching me draw. "That's really good," she says in almost a whisper, like she isn't sure she really wants to say that out loud.

"Thank you," I tell her. "It looks really hard to make those."

Macy shrugs and twirls the bunny around once, then says, "Not really; it just takes practice." She points at my sketchbook and asks, "Can I borrow a piece?"

I tear out a fresh sheet of paper and hand it to her. I watch her fold one corner over like the top of a triangle, and then she folds the bottom part up and down over the edge of the table and rips the end of the paper in a perfectly straight line. "You have to start with a square," she explains, and I have to lean in so that I can hear her because she's talking so quietly.

She makes fold after fold. "Those will be the ears," she tells me, "and this part will pop out and become the tail." I watch as the bunny comes to life right in front of me. Last, she shapes the ears to be floppy just like real bunny ears.

"Wow," I say as she hands it to me.

"You can have it," she mumbles, adding, "I mean, if you want."

"Really? Are you sure?" I ask.

She nods and takes one final sip of juice from her tray. "It's your paper, so . . ." but she doesn't finish. Instead, she stands to take her lunch tray up to the front of the cafeteria.

I admire my new little origami bunny, and while I wait for her to return to the table, I have a thought. I open my sketchbook to the drawing I had just done, and I carefully tear the page out (though not with as straight of a line as Macy's).

When Macy gets back to her seat, I slide the drawing toward her and say, "Here, then you should have this."

She takes the paper from me and gazes admiringly at the drawing. "Thanks."

# Chapter 9

# MATH AND MUSIC

The bell rings. Macy and I walk close together in the sea of students rushing for the cafeteria doors, getting bumped and poked like we're inside a giant pinball machine as we try to get out.

The halls outside are flooded too, with the fourth graders now making their way to the lunchroom. Usually, it's easy to peel away and head down the hallway toward the Resource Room, which is in the opposite direction of our class. Because usually, nobody pays attention to me.

But not today.

I slow my pace, letting Macy get several steps ahead of me. At the intersection of the two hallways, I stop. It feels wrong to just walk away without saying anything. But on the other hand, what am I supposed to say?

Macy glances back when she realizes I'm no longer by her side. "Coming?" she asks.

"I . . ." I'm at a loss for words. LDs and IEPs and Resource Rooms are not noisy-hallway conversation topics to talk about with someone who might not even be an actual friend yet. "I have a . . ." I rack my brain for an excuse. "A *lesson*," I blurt out, pointing down the hall, which happens to be where not only the Resource Room is located, but where the music rooms are as well.

After all, there are a few kids in our class who are learning instruments for band and orchestra. They sometimes leave class for music lessons. Why couldn't I be one of them too? I *am* getting lessons, just not in music. So maybe it's not the worst kind of lie.

"Oh. Okay." Macy pauses. "Well, see you, I guess," she finally says, and gives me a small wave.

I wave back, but as I watch her walk away, there's a pang of guilt knotting up around my throat. I swallow hard and call out, "See you!" but I don't think she hears me.

The Resource Room is not the worst place to be—even if I don't like the fact that I have to come here. There are beanbag chairs and a colorful rug in the center of the room. Lots of decorations everywhere, and posters on the walls that say things like PROGRESS, NOT PERFECTION! and MISTAKES ARE PROOF THAT YOU ARE TRYING and IF YOU THINK YOU CAN, YOU WILL.

"Sadie, Sadie, Sadie!" Mr. Patel calls when I enter the room, which is the way he greets me every time, like I'm on a game show. "Come on down!"

He waves his arms dramatically, gesturing for me to take a seat.

I sit at the table, and he flops a manila file folder down. On the tab, it reads MITCHELL-ROSEN, SADIE (5TH GRADE).

"Let's see what we have here," Mr. Patel mutters, flipping through the pages in the folder. He is always chewing cinnamon gum, and secretly offers me a piece— even though gum chewing is against school rules.

"I have your quiz from last week," he says, holding a piece of paper but not letting me see the grade. "I thought we could go over some of the problems again together."

"The ones I got *wrong*, you mean."

Mr. Patel gives me a *look*—he doesn't like when I say things about bad grades or feeling stupid—and corrects me, "The ones that were more difficult for you is what I meant."

He covers the test with another paper, so that I can only see one problem at a time—a trick I always seem to forget when I'm on my own.

I chew my gum and listen to Mr. Patel. Slowly, math begins to makes sense for a few minutes. Too bad it all falls apart whenever I leave this room and have to take a test or do my homework without him talking me through each step.

If it wasn't for the fact that Mr. Patel is a math teacher, he probably would be my favorite teacher I've ever had. He's patient, unlike Ms. Avery, and even if I judge myself sometimes, he never does.

When I get back to my classroom, just in time for *more math*, it feels like everyone is watching me as I make my way to my seat, even though I do my best to stick to the walls and not make any noise. Bailey crinkles her nose at me like I smell or something. But if I do, it's the cinnamon gum I forgot to spit out before leaving the Resource Room, and nothing gross.

As I sit down, I wonder if they know where I've really been, or if they think I'm just a regular music student learning about the violin or clarinet or something.

## Chapter 10

# WORD PROBLEMS

Last year, I used to go to Jude's house after school. But this year, I'm usually home alone for at least an hour or two until one of my moms gets in. When I get home, the front door is unlocked. That's when I remember: Gramps is here.

As I open the door, I have this dreamy sort of vision that comes into my mind like a movie: Dewey bounding through the house to come greet me, the sound of her paws scrambling against the floor, her tail thwacking against the walls, and then her jumping up on me, so happy that I'm home. It's just a flash, and it ends almost as quickly as it came to me, the room returning to its calm, quiet state.

I close the door behind me and call out, "Gramps, I'm home."

I hear Gramps's voice from the kitchen yell back, "I'm in here."

He is making PB&J sandwiches and has three different kinds of bread out on the counter along with the peanut butter and jar of strawberry jelly, and he says, "Pick your poison." Confusion must show on my face because he adds, "Wheat, rye, or . . . gluten free?" He sticks out his tongue as he holds up the last option.

"Oh. Rye," I tell him, setting my backpack down and taking a seat at the table.

"Good choice."

He hums while I watch him fix the sandwich, and again I start to doubt whether Moms are right about Gramps needing to be taken care of—he's taking care of me right now, isn't he? And last night when I thought he called me by Mom's name, maybe I really did misunderstand him. *Katie* and *Sadie* do sort of sound a lot alike, if you look at them as just two words.

"How was school today?" he asks, as he brings two of his famous PB&J sandwiches to the table. "What'd ya learn?"

"Long. And not much," I answer. "But something interesting did happen. Gramps, do you remember about the girl who hates me?"

He sits down next to me, squints at his sandwich, and says, "Don't tell me . . . Missy?"

"Close. Macy."

"Ah. Macy," he repeats. "She's not giving you grief again, is she?"

"No," I tell him, and I reach down into my backpack to retrieve the origami bunny. "She actually gave me this today." I hold it out for Gramps to take. "She made it."

He turns it around to examine it from all sides. "Gee, that's really something." He sets it down on the table in between us and says, "What brought on this change?"

"Mama told me if I just kept trying to be nice to her that she would come around, and I don't know, I think maybe she finally is." I take a big bite of my sandwich—Gramps's PB&J sandwiches may just be rivaling French toast as my new favorite food.

Gramps takes a bite of his sandwich too, but then holds up his finger while he chews and swallows, like he just thought of something. "Or maybe it's the opposite," he begins. "Maybe *you're* the one who's finally coming around." Gramps always has a way of saying things that makes me think about them in a different way.

I finish my sandwich and take out my homework.

Math.

Gramps is at the sink doing dishes, humming his usual tune, and I am stuck on the very first word problem.

I press the point of my pencil into my notebook so hard that the graphite tip breaks off completely. "Aghh!"

I groan. I slam the pencil into the binding of the note-book and flip the cover closed, letting my head fall into my hands. "I can't do this!"

"No, no, no," Gramps immediately says, shaking his head as he dries his hands on the dish towel. "There's no such thing as *I can't*. I thought you knew better than that."

"Not when it comes to math, Gramps."

"You know, your mother used to struggle with math too," he tells me. "And we had to figure out a way to make sense of it—that's all. Like she said, everybody learns dif-ferently."

"I thought Mom was really good at math in school," I say. "I mean, she had to be to go through all the years of college to be a vet."

"She *was* good at it, but that doesn't mean it was easy for her." He sits down at the table and turns my math book around so it's facing him. "Let's just take a look-see, shall we?" He pats his shirt and pulls his glasses out of the pocket where they always are, then unfolds the arms and loops one over each ear. "Which one are we stuck on?"

I point to number one.

"Delilah made boysenberry jam and strawberry jam. She made enough boysenberry jam to fill one-fourth of a jar," he begins, reading the question out loud. "If she made one-half as much strawberry jam as boysenberry jam, how much strawberry jam does she have?"

"Who cares?" I answer, throwing my hands up.

Gramps ignores me and opens my notebook and picks up the pencil.

"Look at it this way," he says as he begins to draw a cylinder in the center of the page, with a little bit of an indented lip, like the screw top of a jar, along with a second one right next to it. He draws a rectangular label across the front of each and, in his tiny, all-caps lettering, labels one *BOYSENBERRY* and the other *STRAWBERRY*. "Here's your two jars of jam, right?"

"Okay," I grumble.

"Read the question again, and tell me how much boysenberry Daisy has."

"Delilah," I correct. "Um. One-fourth of a jar."

He turns the notebook toward me and says, "Good. And if we want to know how much one-fourth of a jar is, why don't we start by splitting this jar into four parts?" Then he draws a line in the middle of both jars, right through the center of the labels. "Right now, there's one-half and one-half, right?"

"Right," I agree.

Then Gramps writes on one side of the jar: *1/2* on the upper section and *1/2* on the lower section. He draws a line to split the top half in half again, and another line to split the bottom half in half. "And now we have four equal parts. How many fourths is it to this line here?" he asks, pointing with the tip of the pencil on the first line.

"One-fourth."

"Yep, and how many fourths here?" he asks, pointing to the second line.

"Two-fourths," I answer.

"Or?" He moves his pencil along the line to the other side where he had written 1/2.

"One-half."

"Absolutely!" he shouts excitedly. "Next," he continues, pointing to the third line.

"Three-fourths." Then *I* point to the final line and say, "Four-fourths."

"Or?" Gramps prompts again.

"One whole?" I answer.

"Mm-hmm," he says, nodding, handing me the pencil. "Now shade in the amount of boysenberry. What was it again, one-fourth?"

I take the pencil from him and shade in one-fourth of the first jar.

"Exactly, now if Daisy—"

"Delilah," I correct again, laughing.

"If *whoever* has the second jar of strawberry jam but it's

filled with only half as much jam as the boysenberry, you tell me how we would figure that out."

I think about it for a minute. "I'm not sure how to explain it, but I think I can draw it."

He nods and says, "That's fine; draw it instead."

I compare the two jars and shade in half the amount in the second jar as I did in the first jar. "Is that it?" I ask.

"It is. Now we just have to turn that picture into a number for your answer."

I divide up the second jar the same way we divided the first one, and as I look at the amount of strawberry I shaded in, I draw four more lines in between the others and count them silently from the bottom up: *One, two, three, four, five, six, seven, eight.* "One . . . eighth?"

"There, you got it, Sass!" Gramps shouts, and claps his hands together. "Go ahead and write that answer down. See, every problem has a solution; you just have to figure out how to figure it out."

It isn't so hard after all, at least not the way Gramps explains it, anyway. He holds his hand up for a high five, and I feel just a little bit proud of myself. I will have to remember to tell Mr. Patel about this—I think it will make him happy for me.

Now if only I could draw my way through the other problem: getting Dewey free.

# Chapter 11

# LAVA

*JUDE: OPERATION EXPLOSION . . .*

*JUDE: Success!*

I have six unread messages waiting for me. Jude attached three pictures of the volcano—before, during, and after the explosion—along with a video of the entire thing. I can tell her dad must be the one holding the phone that's recording the video because it isn't centered and keeps shaking. But I can still manage to see everything if I tilt my head.

Jude's mountain is made of papier-mâché, and she's painted it to look like a real mountain, with browns and green for grass toward the bottom, and white on the top for snow. There are even fake trees and a blue-painted river moat surrounding the base of the mountain. I can hear her muffled voice explaining as she pours water and drops of dish soap and red and orange food coloring into the top of the volcano, next adding spoonfuls of baking soda. Finally, she pauses and says that once she pours in the last ingredient (vinegar), it is going to set off a chemical reaction. She says something about carbon dioxide gas, but you can't hear because that's when the eruption begins, and it is bigger and foamier and bubblier than her practice volcanoes ever were.

There are all kinds of *whoa*-ing and *wow*-ing and clapping in the background as the lava flows down the sides of the mountain and funnels down into the moat.

> ME: ahh, that looks so awesome!!!

> ME: i wish I could've been there to see it!

Jude is typing . . .

JUDE: you're there! I'm so sorry it's taken me so long to write back! I've been soooo busy!

Jude keeps writing with exclamation points, and it reminds me of when she would be talking about something and get really excited. Her dad would always say she was hyperactive, but she preferred the term *hyperhappy*.

> ME: did you see my message about gramps?

JUDE: Yes, I did. I feel so bad. How does he seem?

ME: idk, he's acting pretty normal now. except
that last night he called me the wrong name.
but other than that, he's just his usual self . . .

JUDE: So he's okay? That's good!

I'm not sure if he's actually okay, because there's still that whole part about how he fell and bumped his head, and that definitely does not seem okay to me. It feels too complicated to talk about in messages right now. So I don't say any of that.

ME: what have you been busy doing?
besides kicking science fair butt?

JUDE: I got invited to my first birthday party in Utah!
That's where I was when you were messaging me
over the weekend. I have FINALLY made some
friends here. Robin and Lark.

JUDE: They're twins.

JUDE: But not the kind that look alike.

ME: oh, wow. I'm so glad.

Except, as I type the words, I feel the air in my bedroom going stale, an inky blackness coiling around my throat. I'm lying to Jude. I'm not glad. But it's not like I can say that.

> ME: i mean not about them being twins
> but about you making fries!

JUDE: mmm, fries ☺

> ME: *friends

JUDE: SO. AM. I. SRSLY!

JUDE: We all go to the same school but we're not in any classes together. We met @ tae kwon do. And they have a cousin Jordie who is in tae kwon do too, who is also pretty cool. I hope you can come visit here over the summer so you can meet them.

JUDE: We played laser tag and I swear that this was the BEST birthday cake I've EVER eaten! You would've loved it. I wish I had a pic . . . It was in the shape of a castle, and the very top of it was made out of real legos. It was yellow cake with white frosting (your favorite) . . . BUT it also had rainbow funfetti stuff inside of it (my favorite) and it was decorated with miniature fake trees and a plastic bridge.

JUDE: It reminded me of our old fairy fortress . . .

I start typing, but then I stop again because I don't want to lie, but it doesn't seem fair to tell Jude how sad it makes me feel that she has Robin and Lark. Especially because I really do want her to have friends in Utah. I swear I do. But now that she does, I wonder if she's going to forget all about me. The thought of that creates a little volcano inside of me now.

JUDE: Hello? Sadie? My dad's calling me to come downstairs. Gotta leave for tae kwon do in like 2 mins!

JUDE: you there?

JUDE: ttyl

ME: I'm really glad you made some new friends. That sounds like a really fun birthday party! I hope I can come over the summer too. I'd love to meet them.

I wait two whole minutes, but my message sits there unread.

I hear a car door close outside. Through my bedroom window, I can see that Mama and Noah just got home. Which means Mom will be home soon too. I need to finish the rest of my math homework before dinner, but as I turn back toward my desk I see the drawing I made of Dewey.

I set aside my lava feelings about Jude and her new friends, because Dewey is counting on me. I need to come up with a plan. And soon. If only there were a way to buy us some more time, or if I could at least convince the shelter that someone is looking for Dewey—that she belongs to someone.

I pick the Dewey drawing up, and I take four tacks from the little container that sits on the corner of my desk and hang my drawing on the wall where I can see it, so I can stay focused on the mission. It comes out crooked, so I have to readjust it a couple of times before it's just right.

"Hey, dweeb, Mama told me to check to see if you finished your homework," Noah says, standing in the doorway of my bedroom.

"Do you mind?" I snap, and spin around to face him with my hands on my hips, trying to block his view of the picture.

"Whatever," he mumbles. He leaves the room, but then he sticks his arm back around the corner and flips my light switch on and off, over and over and over, just to be a butthead.

"Hey!" I yell.

Of course, he leaves with the light *off*. I walk across the room to turn my light back on and close the door. As I stand back and see the way the picture looks hanging up on the wall—like a poster—an idea strikes.

I sit down with my laptop, and I search for photos of dogs. I find one of a German shepherd that has a different face, but the same kind of fluffy coat as Dewey's. The German shepherd is sitting in a grassy, bright, fenced-in backyard, with its mouth open in a big doggy smile, sitting next to a kid who has their arm around it. Next, I open up my internet browser and go to the shelter's website. I click on the link *Lost & Found Pets*, and I scroll through pages of cats and dogs until I find Dewey's picture. It's not a great one. She looks scared, sitting in the corner of her kennel at the shelter with the saddest eyes I've ever seen. But I copy the picture and paste it into the poster.

I use the tracing tool to cut out the background, and instead I place Dewey's face in the picture of the grassy yard on the German shepherd's body, with the kid's arm around her. She looks happier already, just being in a different setting. I touch it up and use some more filters and blending tools, and I zoom in so you can't see the kid's face, just their arm around the body of the other dog, which now has Dewey's head. I can't quite get the fur colors to match, so I flip it to black and white instead of color and . . . it works.

Next, I search for the right template.

>Posters

>>Lost and Found

I drop in the doctored Dewey photo in the square that takes up most of the page. In a big font I type the words *LOST DOG*, and then underneath that, in smaller lettering, I write: *Her name is Dewey, and her family misses her very much! REWARD! If found, please call* . . .

I hadn't thought my plan through this far. I need to add a phone number, but it can't be mine or anyone else's number that Mom would be able to recognize. That rules out anyone in our family. And Jude too. I can't just make up a number either, because if I show it to Mom, she's definitely going to call. I'll need someone on the outside who can help: an accomplice.

But I'll have to deal with that part later.

Aside from the phone number problem, and the fact that, of course, there is no reward, or family, I have to say this poster looks real. The poster will be proof that someone, somewhere, is looking for Dewey.

For now, I'm starting to feel a tiny little spark of hope that maybe there is something I can do about this, even if I am a kid.

Someone knocks on my door. I click on the X in the corner of my window, quickly whip out my math homework, and pick up a pencil so it looks like I'm working. "Come in."

"Dinner's ready, Sassafras," Gramps says as he opens

my door. "How's that math homework treating you?" he asks.

I look down at my notebook. "Not so great," I admit, hoping he doesn't notice I never even made it through the second problem. "I got distracted," I tell him. Gramps walks in and looks over my shoulder at my homework.

"You can do it, just like we worked through the first one. But *after* dinner," he adds.

I stand up and start toward the door, and I hear Gramps say, "Gee, that's really something."

I turn around and see that Gramps is holding the origami rabbit in the palm of his hand.

"Where'd this come from?" he asks.

At first I think he's joking—we just had this conversation downstairs—but he's looking at me, waiting for an answer. Before I can say anything, Mom sticks her head in my room and says, "Dinner's ready, you guys."

Gramps sets the rabbit in its place on my desk, and sings back, "We're coming, we're coming. Hold your horses."

## Chapter 12

# CODE NAME: ACCOMPLICE

I am late for the bus the next morning because I forget my (unfinished) math homework on my desk and have to run back home for it. Thankfully I make it to the bus right before the doors close. I walk down the aisle, and it feels like everyone is staring at me.

The farther back I walk the more worried I become that no one is going to let me sit with them. Even the kids who don't have anyone sitting next to them scoot to the edge of their seats so I can't sit down. Finally, toward the middle of the bus, on the right side, I see Macy. Normally I would completely avoid eye contact with her, but today I don't. And when I get to her seat, she doesn't glare at me. She slides toward the window and pulls her backpack onto her lap.

I sit down and tell her, "Thanks."

She nods and murmurs, "Mm-hmm."

It's really nice to have someone to sit next to for a change, even if that someone isn't particularly talkative. It's not until the bus drops us off and we're walking toward the school that Macy speaks. "We could sit together later, too—if you want."

I'm not sure if she's talking about later on the bus after school or later at lunch, but I just say, "Okay," because either way, that sounds good to me.

Maybe Gramps was right about Macy and me—I start to wonder if it was me who needed to come around. Or maybe she forgot that she was supposed to hate me. If I don't have to worry about being her archenemy, that's one big concern off my mind. And having one less thing to worry about would be a very good thing right now.

At my desk, my thoughts drift to Dewey, all sad and alone in that cold crate in the back room of the shelter, and a shiver runs through my body. I concentrate on her and how much I already love her, and then I fix my mind on the one clear thought I want her to know: *I haven't forgotten you, Dewey; I'm working on getting you out.*

I think back to when we first met in the woods, how she gave me her paw, and then I imagine us walking together back toward the house, except this time Noah doesn't scare her away with his big mouth. We go into the backyard together, and I close the gate behind us and I tell Dewey, "We're home." I watch her run after the birds in the yard, and then I realize I'm laughing out loud.

The classroom comes back into focus.

Ms. Avery said something. Everyone is taking out their English books and opening them up. I turn around in my seat to see if I can tell what page the book of the kid behind me is open to, but they pull it closer to them, like I'm cheating or something.

The student in front of me begins reading out loud. My stomach starts to ache, my heart punches inside my chest—I wasn't paying attention again, and now it's almost my turn. I'm turning the pages, trying to find where we are, when Macy tilts her open book toward me and whispers, "Top of page seventy-three."

When it gets to my turn, I'm able to pick up where the last reader left off without Ms. Avery needing to skip over me this time, which is supposed to take the pressure off me but mostly makes me worried that the other students will notice the special treatment.

"Good," Ms. Avery says, looking satisfied when I finish my passage.

I glance across the aisle at Macy and mouth, *Thank you.*

She tosses an origami triangle onto my desk.

I open it and read:

*You're welcome. I meant to ask if you ever found
the dog you were telling me about. I looked for it
on my way to the bus stop this morning but I didn't
see it.*

I write back under her note:

*thx for asking about the dog. her name is Dewey, btw.
I found her but ~~she's still in danger.~~*

I debate what I can (or should) tell her about the
Dewey mission. Saying she's in danger might seem a little
strange, so I cross that out.

*~~but she's stuck at the animal shelter.~~*

Except "stuck at the shelter" isn't really accurate either,
though, so I scribble that out too.

*but it's a long story. I could tell you about it at lunch
if you want???*

I toss the note back over to Macy—she reads it and
makes the *okay* sign with her hand. And then she immediately begins reading out loud from the text. I hadn't even
noticed it was getting to her turn. I don't know how she
manages to pay attention all the time. Maybe if we ever
become real friends, I can ask her.

*✳ ✳ ✳*

**In the cafeteria,** I unpack my lunch bag at the seat at the end of the table where Macy always sits, while I wait for her to get through the lunch line. The longer I sit there alone, the more I wonder if she'll really sit down next to me.

Then, finally, after what feels like an entire hour, I see Macy walking toward me, carrying her lunch tray. She sits in the seat next to me and opens up her carton of juice. She sticks her straw in and takes a big sip.

It's only then that she looks at me and says, "What's the long story?"

"Well," I begin, and tell her everything—except that Dewey and I can talk to each other.

"Maybe someone will claim her?" Macy offers.

I shake my head. "They won't. I can't explain how I know, but I just do."

We're quiet for a while, and I finally start eating my cold leftover veggie pizza while Macy finishes her grilled cheese and dips her spoon into the Styrofoam bowl of tomato soup.

Macy sets her spoon down in the bowl and leans toward me. "Wait, but I adopted Dango from the animal shelter—that's my rabbit." She looks at me, waiting for a response, but when I don't say anything she goes on. "I mean, why can't they just wait for someone to adopt the dog if she doesn't have anyone?"

"I thought of that too. I even begged my moms to let *me* adopt her, because I know she's such a good—such a great, special, *amazing*—dog. But they said no."

"Your mom*s*?" Macy asks, emphasis on the *s*, so I know her question is about the plural part.

"Yeah," I tell her. "I have two moms."

"Oh," Macy says, but I can't tell what she's thinking.

So I say, "Families come in all shapes, sizes, and colors," repeating something Moms have been telling Noah and me since as far back as I can remember.

Whenever I say that, I always think back to this one picture that we took that hangs on my moms' bedroom wall. It's all of our hands in a circle, with our fingers almost touching. Mama's light, freckled complexion, like the pale pink of rose petals; Mom's always-smooth, rich-umber-and-sepia skin; with me and Noah in the middle, gold and sand, like shades of a rainbow.

I start to get impatient, wondering if I should just get up and go back to my old spot at the other end of the table. Maybe Macy is just one of those people who doesn't understand. But finally, after a long pause, she says, "Well, I don't have *any* moms, so I think you're pretty lucky to have two."

"I've never thought about it like that," I tell her, but her eyes suddenly have this faraway look, like she's thinking about something. "Why don't you have a mom?" I wonder out loud. "I mean, if that's okay to ask?"

Macy squirms in her seat and shakes her head. "I don't really wanna talk about it."

"Okay," I say.

There's a pause, but Macy comes back to the conversation. "I do have a dad, and my grandma—my sobo, I call her." She explains, "That's 'grandmother' in Japanese."

"Gramps—that's what I call my grandpa," I offer. "He just moved in with us."

She nods and smiles like she understands.

I kind of want to ask her more questions, like what's it like to have a dad and a grandma, or does her grandma have trouble remembering things and get confused at night too? But I'm sure those are the kinds of questions that Moms would say are too personal or rude to ask someone you barely know, so I keep talking about Dewey instead.

"They think she's mean and dangerous because of how she was acting at the shelter, but she's not," I say, instead of asking any of those too-personal questions. "She was just scared. But I'm going to find a way to get her out of there, I just don't exactly know how." I reach into my backpack to pull out the flyer I worked on last night. "I'm calling it Code Name: Lost and Found."

Macy reads the flyer and rubs the picture of Dewey with her finger like she's petting her head.

"I thought if I could make a 'lost dog' poster and give it to my mom to bring to the shelter, it could at least buy her some more time," I continue. "But I don't have a phone number to include, so I don't think that will work either."

"She's adorable," Macy coos, still touching Dewey's face in the picture. "I wish I could adopt her."

"Wait a minute," I say, wheels turning in my brain. "What if you *could* adopt her?"

Macy narrows her eyes at me and says, "I thought you said she couldn't be adopted?"

"No, I mean what if we could convince the animal shelter that Dewey is really your dog? That she was always your dog and that you've been looking for her? We could put your phone number on the flyer—it's perfect!"

"But my dad's allergic to dogs, so I could never take her home even if we could convince them." I feel all the air in my lungs deflate like a balloon. "But . . ." Macy begins, "you could use my phone number on the flyer if you want. I mean, if you think it would help."

"Really?" I shout. I'm so happy, I want to throw my arms around Macy.

She writes her phone number across the empty space on the flyer.

"So if they call you, you'll say that Dewey is yours?" I double-check.

Macy nods. She leans over the paper and reads it more closely before crossing out the middle of the word *reward*. I had typed "REWRAD" in my excitement. She rewrites it: *REWARD*.

"Thanks," I tell her.

She just shrugs and says, "I'll keep thinking of ideas. I mean, we have to do something."

*We.* I like the sound of that.

## Chapter 13

# BUTTERFLYER

I race home from the bus stop after school, yelling, "I'm home, Gramps!" as I run up the stairs to my bedroom. I drop my backpack on the floor next to my desk and swing my laptop open. I type in the wrong password twice because I'm too excited—*hyperhappy*, as Jude would say.

The third time works.

I open up the poster file, pull the folded paper Macy wrote her phone number on out of my back pocket, and carefully type in the number. I proofread everything in the poster once more. I change "REWRAD" to "REWARD" and make the heading even larger. I click save, then print.

I nearly fall down the stairs to make it to the printer because I'm running too fast. I race past Gramps in the kitchen, and he says, "Where's the fire?"

"What?" I yell from the little office nook area in the living room, where we have a computer that Moms use to do grown-up things like pay bills and stuff like that. The poster has just finished printing as I skid to a stop in front of the desk.

"What's the hurry?" he says, translating his Gramps-speak for me.

"Nothing," I tell him, careful to keep the paper facing me. "I just had to get some homework off the printer."

"Okey dokey. You want a snack while you do your homework?"

"If it's your famous PB&J, then yes!"

"Oh, they're famous now, are they?" Gramps laughs and says, "Coming right up."

"BRB," I tell him.

This time Gramps says, "Say what?"

"BRB, Gramps. Be right back. You know: *Bee. Are. Bee.* Get it?"

He nods and says, "BRH."

"What's that?"

"Be. Right. Here. See, I'm still young and hip."

"I know that, Gramps."

Back in my room I look at the Dewey drawing hanging on my wall, with its four tacks holding it in place. I set the freshly printed poster on my desk. And then I take a new tack from the little container on my desk and poke a tiny hole in all four corners of the poster. If I'm going to convince Moms, it has to look real.

✳ ✳ ✳

**I come downstairs** before dinner; Mom and Mama are in the kitchen talking while they cook. I don't even bother asking if we're having breakfast for dinner. I can barely remember what our special French toast even tastes like, but now is not the time to mention that.

"Hi, sweetness," Mama says when she notices me standing there.

"Hi, Moms."

Mom turns around and asks, "How was school?"

"Meh," I say with a shrug.

"Meh?" she repeats. "Yeah, my day was kind of *meh* too."

"But"—I clear my throat, which has suddenly turned dry as dust, my pulse drumming in my ears—"look what I found on the way home from school, Mom!" I hold out the poster with the four pinholes in the corners and the wrinkles and creases I made by putting it in and pulling it out of my backpack over and over again, and hope that no one notices the way my hands are shaking—like they do whenever I try to lie about something.

Mom holds the paper up in front of her face, so I can't see what kind of an expression she's making. "Hmm," is all she says. I place my hand over my chest, feeling my heart pounding under my fingertips. Does she believe the poster is real?

109

Am I caught? Should I just confess and get it over with?

Mama comes to look at the poster too. "Where'd you find this, honey?"

"It was on a tree—or a—a post, a light pole, I mean. Near the bus stop." I fumble. I hadn't thought of the answer to that question. "It's her, isn't it? The dog from the shelter?" I ask, even though I already know it is (with a few minor touch-ups).

"Hmm," Mom mutters again. "It certainly does *look* like her."

Noah bounds into the room and leans over the counter, squinting at the poster upside down, and says, "That is one weird-looking dog."

"She's a beautiful, unique-looking dog."

"She *is*," Mama agrees. "Very unique."

"What are we looking at?" Gramps says as he comes into the room.

"Sadie found a lost-dog poster today," Mama answers.

Now the entire family is staring at the poster I made, and I start to get a little tingle in my fingers, a familiar queasy feeling in my stomach. As Gramps leans over to get a closer look at it, he meets my eyes and sort of squints at me and turns his head, almost like he's trying to telepathically communicate something to *me*. It's a look that makes me wonder if he's figured out that this was the thing I had printed out just that afternoon.

I start to worry he might say something, but just then, Catniss jumps up on the counter and sits herself right down on top of the paper. She stretches out her front leg and starts licking her paw, then draws it over her face again and again.

*Perfect timing*, I try my telepathy on Catniss.

In response, Catniss yawns in that way that shows her tiny sharp teeth, making her look like a miniature tiger.

"Catniss," Mom scolds, "the kitchen counter is not a place to take a bath."

Mom pulls the sheet of paper out from under the cat. Catniss meows and it sounds like she's whining "Mo-oo-om" just like a real human kid would.

I silently thank Catniss for creating a diversion.

Mom pulls her phone out of her pocket, looking back and forth between the phone and the paper as she dials the number. I hold my breath as I hear ringing through the other end. It rings once, twice, three times—*Macy, pick up*—four times, and then, "He-hello?"

"Hello," Mom says. "I'm with the county animal shelter, and I'm calling about a lost dog notice that I saw for Dewey. I think we may have her."

I can't tell exactly what Macy is saying, but I can hear her voice muffled through the phone.

"Okay, well, is there a grown-up I could speak with?" Mom says, and after a few seconds continues, "They're busy right now? All right, well, do you think you could ask them to give us a call back at the shelter tomorrow? Great, can you write down this phone number—I'll wait. Okay, it's five, five, five . . ."

Macy did it!

"You're welcome," Mom says into the phone, smiling warmly. "I'm glad we found her too. Okay, goodbye."

She really did it!

"Well?" Mama prompts.

"It sounds like this dog belongs to them."

"That's great!" I shout.

"Wait a minute." Mom scrunches up her forehead. "Why are you so happy about *that*—I thought you wanted to adopt her?"

"But you said we can't, right?" I double-check, just in case.

"That's right."

"So if we can't have her . . ." I pause, thinking fast. "Then I'm glad she's at least going to be reunited with her family."

"That's very sweet, honey," Mama says, and then she gives Mom one of her *looks*. "Wouldn't you say that's a pretty mature attitude?"

"It is." Mom sets the poster back down and Catniss immediately curls up on top of it again. "Very mature, Sadie," she says, with a nod of approval.

Noah scoops Catniss off of the counter and whispers, "Yeah, mature for a toddler" into Catniss's ear as he carries her into the living room.

Noah sets Catniss down on the couch and bounds up the stairs, but I stay behind.

"So, Mom, what's going to happen to Dewey now?" I ask.

"I'll let the shelter know that she has an owner, and we'll figure out a time for them to come and pick her up." She smiles at me. "I'm proud of you for being so grown up about this. And I love how much you care about this dog, Sadie. I mean it."

"She's a good egg," Gramps says, picking up the poster and looking at it more closely.

I only feel relieved for a few seconds before I realize that this was just the first step. When no one comes to pick up Dewey, then won't she be back in the same place? The poster has only bought me some time to figure out what to do next.

Up in my room I unzip the little pocket on the inside of my backpack and pull out my phone, which is only supposed to be used for emergencies, "*real emergences*," and never during school. Which means that technically I'm not breaking any rules: I am not at school, and if Dewey's predicament doesn't qualify as a real emergency, then I don't know what does.

I text Jude in all caps, one word: BUTTERFLYER.

Once, back in our fairy-fortress days, Gramps was playing with us in the backyard; he picked up the butterfly magnet that we'd added to the fairy community—it had shimmery plastic wings that could actually flutter—and making it soar all around the tree, he shouted, "Mayday!" Gramps dubbed it the "Butterflyer," and he told us that *Mayday* is the word that pilots would use over the radio when they were in trouble and needed help. It's "Mayday" because it sounds like a different word in French that means "help me."

Well, I'm having a major Mayday moment. Also known as a "butterflyer" between Jude and me, and we reserve it for only the direst situations. Like life-and-death seriousness. I didn't even use a butterflyer when everything was happening at the beginning of the school year with all the testing and the meetings and the IEP.

Butterflyer moments were used for things like: When I broke my arm last year. When Jude's parents told her they were getting a divorce. Then when Jude found out she was moving. When I thought I was going to die of loneliness that first week of school without her (or that Macy was going to beat me up).

While I wait for Jude's response, I get up to close my bedroom door and then I turn on the light in my closet and sit on the floor, pulling all the clothes in around me like patchwork curtains. I imagine Jude, all the way in Utah, doing the same thing: making her way to her own bedroom, pushing the hangers aside, settling in to dispense some biffle advice and comfort.

It's been four minutes.

"Jude, come on," I say out loud, like maybe I can telepathically call to her all the way across the five states that currently separate us.

Seven minutes.

I decide to call her instead—maybe she just didn't see my text come in.

It rings and rings and rings. Until a generic voicemail robot answers, telling me that Jude is not available. "What!" I say out loud to my shirts and sweaters hanging all around me.

*BEEP.*

"Jude, hey," I whisper into the phone. "Listen, it's a butterflyer over here. Call me as soon as you get this message. Oh, it's me, your biffle."

Three more minutes pass before my phone vibrates in

my hand and its glow illuminates the darkened closet. But it's not a phone call from Jude. It's a text.

All it says is: hi, sry. will call u back later. robin & lark r here right now

**It's not until** the numbers on my alarm clock change from 11:22 to 11:23 that I admit the truth: Jude is not going to call me back tonight.

And even though I should be tired, I've never been more wide-awake.

"Dewey?" I say out loud.

I close my eyes and listen hard to my thoughts.

Nothing. All I hear are the sounds of the house. Noah's snoring down the hall. Moms' TV in their bedroom, the muffled voice of a news anchor. But underneath all of those, I hear the sound of dishes being pulled out of the cupboard.

I make my way downstairs to find that Gramps has a steaming mug set out in his usual spot at the kitchen table. And he's at the counter, making himself a PB&J sandwich for a midnight snack.

"Hiya, Sass, you're up late."

I sit at the kitchen table and sigh. "Mm-hmm."

"You want half of this?" he asks.

"No thanks," I murmur. "Not hungry."

"Why so glum, chum?" He glances over his shoulder and asks, "Math homework gotcha down again?"

"No, it's not that."

Gramps sits down with his PB&J and takes a bite, looking up at me. "I'm happy to lend an ear, Sassafras . . . ?"

I shrug, not wanting to add to Gramps's worries.

Gramps nods and goes to the refrigerator. But instead of opening it, he pulls a paper from under a magnet and brings it back with him, sitting down once again. He slides the lost and found flyer across the table so that it's facing me.

"Did you want to talk about where this poster *really* came from?" he asks me.

I swallow hard, past a big lump sticking in my throat. "You know?" I croak.

"I know," he confirms.

"I just wanted to make it seem like someone was looking for Dewey," I explain. "So that she has more time." Gramps nods, encouraging me to keep talking. "I already knew she was in trouble because she *told* me so at the shelter the other day. And so I had to do something."

"I have one question," Gramps finally says, and I clench my stomach muscles, preparing to be scolded by the one person I've never wanted to disappoint. "So, if this poster is a fake, who was your mother talking with on the phone tonight?"

"It—it's Macy's number," I stutter—that wasn't the question I was expecting. "She said I could use it; she wants to help too."

"Origami Macy?" he asks.

"Yes! Exactly, Gramps—Origami Macy!" I smile, knowing that Gramps does remember her. "But the thing is she can't actually adopt Dewey."

"I don't want you to worry about the dog," he tells me—*easier said than done*. "I'm on it. We're not going to let anything bad happen to Marshmallow, honey."

"Marshmallow?" I repeat. "You mean . . . Dewey, right?"

"Right." He stands up and carries the mug over to my side of the table, setting it down in front of me. "Here, I made this for you."

I peer into the mug. It smells like flowers. "What is it?" I ask.

"It's your favorite: chamomile with just a spoonful of honey." He scrunches his forehead as he looks at me, like *I'm* confusing *him*. "To help you get back to sleep," he clarifies.

My favorite is hot chocolate with whipped cream. *Mom's* favorite is chamomile. "Oh. Um, thank you," I say.

"Of course, silly." He chuckles, adding, "What are fathers for?"

"Grandfathers," I whisper. But he doesn't hear me.

"Now you get back into bed before Mommy finds out we've been out here having fun without her."

I've never once called either of my moms Mommy—because Mom always said that was the name she reserved for her mother when she was young.

"Gramps?"

He has his back to me, busy clearing his plate and bringing it to the sink.

"Off you go," he tells me.

So I stand with my mug of tea that I didn't ask for, and walk toward the stairs. I turn around in the doorway and call his name one last time. *"Gramps!"*

He turns around and looks at me then. "Yeah, Sass?"

"Nothing. Just—good night."

"Sleep tight," he whispers.

## Chapter 14

# STICKS AND STONES

The sound of my alarm clock is the worst noise in the entire world, which is why I can't figure out why I would press the snooze button so many times. I want to keep sleeping, but then I have to hear the blasted buzzing over and over again!

On the tenth time I hit snooze, Mama swings my bedroom door open. "Sadie!" She doesn't sound happy. I open one eye. She doesn't *look* happy either. Hands on hips, scrunched face. "You need to get up!"

"Five more minutes," I mumble, and turn over, pulling the covers up over my head.

Next thing I know: *BEEP. BEEP. BEEP. BEEP.*

I slam the alarm clock until the noise stops.

Before I even have a chance to get comfy again, the blankets are pulled right off me.

My eyelids fly open.

"*Arrrgh*, Noah!" I shout, jumping out of bed. "Moms!"

"Someone woke up on the wrong side of the bed this morning," he mutters.

"Gee, I wonder why?"

"*Grumpelstiltskin*," he teases, using that word they used to call me when I was little and I would get into a bad mood. It's just another way for him to call me "toddler" without it sounding quite as mean.

"Noah, you are an ugly jerk-head, butt-face dork, and I cannot stand you!"

Of course, *that* is the exact moment Moms show up.

"Sadie," Mama gasps. "Do not call your brother names like that!"

"But he called me—ugh, never mind!" I pick my blankets up off the floor, muttering under my breath.

"What?" Mom asks, coming in my room to help me spread the comforter out over my bed. "What did he call you, Sadie? I'm listening."

"Grumpelstiltskin."

Mom starts laughing, but Mama gives her one of those teacher looks of hers and Mom quickly covers her mouth. "Sorry, Sade—it's just, you do seem a little grumpel— *grumpy*, I mean."

**I'm out the** door in record time.

When I get to the bus stop, Macy isn't there. I wait, but by the time the bus pulls up she still hasn't arrived. No one talks to me the entire ride to school. Which is fine with me. My head is all fizzy and floaty. I don't even remember falling asleep last night. My mind just kept running through the list of things (or people) I'm worried about right now:

Gramps.

Dewey.

Jude.

On repeat.

I cross my arms over my stomach and stare out the window, my eyelids so heavy, that lump in my throat re-appearing. I wish I were home right now, snuggled up in my bed with Dewey.

I close my eyes and imagine it, in as much detail as I can, like I'm drawing it in my mind: Dewey's doggy smile and soft, fluffy fur; her tail wagging as we tumble out of bed and go downstairs for a magnificent French toast breakfast followed by a walk through the enchanted woods, and she'd translate for me what all the forest animals were saying, and I'd be like a cooler version of Snow White (except minus the poison apple/Prince Charming/evil stepmother junk).

With all the woodland creatures as my friends and Dewey as my very best friend, I wouldn't even need people anymore!

*People, how boring!* I imagine saying to Dewey, and then all the other animals would join in the laughter too, once Dewey translated what I'd said.

"Wake up, Spacegirl!" a voice yells in my ear.

My eyes fly open, and I can't tell if I had dreamed the voice or if it really happened. I look up and see that the aisle is already filling with kids standing, waiting to disembark the bus. I meet Jayden's eyes and they're staring at me like maybe I am an alien.

"What?" he snaps.

I can't think of anything to say, except maybe growl because I'm so mad and sad and grumpy, but that would only make him think I was even more of a weirdo, so I clench my teeth and wait until everyone else files out before I get off the bus. Maybe Macy was having one of these grumpelstiltskin days on the first day of school and that's why she growled. I get that now.

Ms. Avery takes attendance and the morning announcements play all the way through, and still no Macy. When Ms. Avery turns around to write something on the board, I sneak my phone out of its pocket in my backpack, but just as I'm about to tap out a message to Macy, I see something move out of the corner of my eye. It's her.

"You weren't at the bus stop this morning," I whisper to her across the aisle as she sits down.

She organizes her things and then holds up her finger, as if to say, *Just a minute.* I watch as she pulls a clean sheet of yellow paper from a folder inside her desk and begins writing. She folds it up quickly, into a triangle, looks up to make sure Ms. Avery isn't watching, and reaches over to place it in my hand.

*Sadie,*

*I'm never at the bus stop on Thursdays (I have a Dr. appt. every week before school on Thursdays). What did your mother say after we got off the phone last night? Did she believe us?? I was awake thinking about it all night!*

*—m.m.m.*

*PS Your mom seems very nice.*

I had noticed that there were some days she didn't ride the bus, but I never paid too much attention to know that it was always Thursday—I was just relieved when she wasn't there. It's funny how things can change so much in such a short amount of time.

Underneath her words, I write:

*OMG! I'm so happy to see you here! I forgot about
Thursdays. ~~But, why do you have to go to the doc so
much? Are you sick?~~ Are you okay? Is that rude of me
to ask? If it is, you don't have to answer . . .*

*Yes, both of my moms believed everything! Thank
you thank you THANK YOU, M.M.M.!* ☺

**It takes ten** eternities to get to lunchtime. We sit at
the end of the cafeteria table: Macy with a container of
noodles and veggies that look *so much better* than yet another day of cold pizza leftovers for me.

"Looks yummy," I tell her as I slip my napkin note from
my lunch bag into my back pocket, hoping Macy doesn't
see. She does kind of glance at what I'm doing, but I'm
too fast for her to see the writing: *Love you always, Sadie!
XOXO, Moms.*

"Sobo's soba," Macy says, grinning. "It's kind of an inside joke. Soba is the kind of noodles. And Sobo is my
grandma? Get it?"

I smile, but it's hard to laugh because Macy mention-
ing her grandma instantly reminds me of Gramps and
how confused he was last night.

"Are you okay?" She asks me the same question I
had asked her in our note. She didn't answer me then,

and now I don't know how to answer her either.

"It's probably nothing," I lie.

"Are you sure?" Macy asks, slurping a bite of her noodles. "Because you're making a face like you're locked in an outhouse trying not to breathe."

The laugh collecting in my lungs forces me to exhale. "Something really weird happened with my gramps last night." I tell her all about our conversation: how he had figured out about the flyer being a fake but said he'd take care of things with Dewey anyway, even though he called her Marshmallow, and then the whole bizarre tea thing.

"I think . . ." I conclude, "I think he thought, for just a minute anyway, that he was my dad and I was my mom, and not just in the saying-the-wrong-name way—it was like he was stuck in a memory or something."

"Wow," Macy breathes. "That's kind of scary."

"Yeah," I agree. "It was, kind of."

We sit in our own bubble of quiet in the middle of the noisy cafeteria, and I start to think, for the first time since Jude left, that maybe I could actually be okay here without her someday.

"Macy?" I finally say, breaking the silence. "Can I tell you something?"

"Sure."

"What happened on the first day of school. On the bus,

I mean. That was a complete accident. I wasn't paying attention. I never would've tripped you on purpose. This whole time I thought you hated me. But then you were the only person who was nice to me after I made a total jerk of myself in class earlier this week. You're kind of the only person who's been nice to me lately at all."

"I'm sorry I was so mean about what happened on the bus. I shouldn't have—it's just that I'm so used to people making fun of me, calling me names . . ."

"Me too!" I admit, beginning to feel a little flutter in my throat, my eyes getting wet. "Which is why I wouldn't do that to anyone else."

"My sobo always says 'sticks and stones'—you know the saying, right?"

"Words can never hurt you?" I finish.

"Yeah." She pauses and looks at me, her chin trembling, and I can't tell if she's about to laugh or cry. "So I try not to get upset about words, but it's not easy."

"I hate that saying," I tell her. "It's applesauce!" She doesn't know that Gramps-ism, but it makes her smile anyway.

"So . . . we're friends, then?" she asks me, uncertainly.

"Friends," I agree.

"Well, then in that case, maybe . . ." She stops short.

"Maybe what?"

"Maybe you could come over to my house after school today?"

I feel all warm and cozy inside, and I actually *want* to go to Macy's house. I want to meet her bunny and her grandma and see what her bedroom is like. Even though it doesn't really help the mission of rescuing Dewey, it still feels like a good idea.

Also, maybe I don't quite want to face Gramps yet. I don't want to know yet what he does or doesn't remember from last night. Macy and I immediately pack up our things and go to one of the lunch monitors to ask to go to the lavatory, not to conduct an "experiment," as Jude would say, but to sneak a phone call to my moms.

Mama, to be exact.

"It's ringing," I whisper to Macy, who is standing in the bathroom stall next to me.

She holds up both hands in between us, with her fingers crossed.

"Sadie?" Mama answers. "Is everything okay?"

"Yes, everything's okay. I was just hoping I'd catch you on a break between classes—and I know, I know I'm only supposed to use my phone in emergencies, and this isn't technically an *emergency*," I say, talking fast before she has a chance to get upset with me. "But I wanted to see if I could go to my friend's house after school because we're working on a project for school that's due, like, soon," I lie. "It's Macy, you know . . . Macy from my class," I add, thinking of how Mama would be proud of me for finally making friends with her.

I wait as she sighs and tells me how I really need to start thinking ahead and managing my time better. She asks questions about whether Macy's parent will be there and where Macy lives and when I'll be home. I remind her that Macy and I wait at the same bus stop so that's proof we live close enough to each other for me to be safe walking. She finally agrees.

Just as I hang up, the bell rings.

Macy and I walk together toward our classroom, but as we approach the spot where those two halls meet, my heart starts to beat faster. I don't want to lie to Macy about where I'm going again.

I stop walking. "Macy, I have—"

"A lesson, right?" she finishes.

Moms would say I have nothing to be embarrassed about—everyone needs extra help with something—and I know even Mr. Patel would agree. But still, I nod and say, "Yeah. A lesson."

## Chapter 15

# M.M.M.

Macy's house is only a few minutes' walk away from the bus stop, and only two streets over from where Jude used to live. I'm surprised I never saw Macy out around the neighborhood before, considering how close she lives.

"Shoes off, shoes off!" is the first thing I hear as I walk into Macy's house. There is a mat next to the door that has several pairs of men's dress shoes, and women's sandals, and even a pair of bunny slippers sitting on it.

Macy drops her backpack to the floor and calls out, "I *know*." She frowns at me, and whispers, "Sorry." She wiggles her sneakers off without untying them and sets them neatly next to the other shoes. So I do the same.

"My moms have tried to institute a no-shoes rule in our house so many times," I tell her. "But everyone's always running around in such a hurry that they start forgetting." I'm rambling. It's always kind of a weird feeling when you go to someone's house for the first time. I guess I must be a little nervous—it's been a really long time since I went to anyone's house for the first time. "It smells nice in here," I continue.

"Thanks," Macy says. "I have to go say hi to my grandma, and introduce you, okay?" She grimaces, like maybe she's just as nervous as I am, like maybe neither of us wants to seem too nerdy, even if we are outside of school.

I follow Macy through a living room and into the kitchen, where her grandma is humming to herself as she rolls out some kind of dough on top of the counter.

"How was school today, Mieko?" her grandma says without looking up from what she's doing. I like the sound of her accent, the way she separates her syllables so they are precise and clean. When I was younger, Mama used to get on me for mumbling, and I would have to practice enunciating my words instead of mashing them together. *To-day*, I repeat in my head.

"Sobo, this is Sadie from—"

Macy starts to say, but as her grandma looks up, she interrupts, "Why did you not say we have company?"

"I was—this is Sadie, from my class," Macy continues.

"*Say-tea*," her grandma repeats, breaking my name into two distinct words, making it sound prettier, more sophisticated. Then, with a big smile: "Welcome; so nice to meet you!"

"Well, we sort of met before," I tell her. "Last year, when you came to our school."

"Oh! Yes, yes, I remember you," she says. That makes me smile, because I often thought about her after her presentation to our class. She just seemed like such a *grandmotherly* grandma—sweet and kind and fair—like I imagined my own grandmothers would have been, had I ever gotten a chance to know them.

"We're working on a project together, Sobo." Macy gives me a tiny secret nod, and I know: she wants me to play along.

"Yeah," I add. "For our social studies class."

Her Grandma immediately goes to the refrigerator, opening the drawers and the freezers, rummaging through. "Go. Go work, Mieko. I will bring snacks."

Macy waves her hand in a quick motion to lead me out of the kitchen. I follow her back out across the living room. "I knew she'd leave us alone if I mentioned schoolwork."

I wonder if Macy feels bad like I do about the little lies.

We pass a big sliding glass door that must lead to the backyard, and there are *tons* of potted plants sitting in the sunlight. When Macy sees me pause to admire them, she stops to let me look closer. "My dad loves to grow things; we always have a garden outside in the summer, and he brings his favorite plants inside when the weather gets cold."

"I love them," I say, cradling a spidery cluster of leaves that are flowing over the sides of one of the pots. "My mom likes having plants in our house, but they always shrivel up."

"Dad says that every plant is different, like every person is different. Some want more water or less sun, or more sun and less water—you just have to get to know them."

"Plants are like people," I repeat. "I like that. Hey, why does your grandma call you Mieko?" I whisper.

"That's my middle name, but she's the only one who calls me that—it's sort of her pet name for me."

"My gramps calls me Sassafras—oh, but that's *not* my middle name!" I'm quick to add. "I have two middle names, actually. Sadie Kathryn Eleanor Mitchell-Rosen. After both of my moms' first names."

"That's sort of like me: Mieko was my great-grandma's name," she says as she picks up a spray bottle from one of the plant stands and spritzes a few of the plants.

"I've always liked that my middle names are bigger than just me," I say. "I don't know, it makes me feel kind of . . ."

"Special?" Macy puts forth.

"Yeah," I agree.

Macy nods and turns a few of the pots toward the sun. "Let's go to my room," she says. "You can meet my bunny."

We go down a hallway and reach a door that has the letters *M.M.M.* cut out of felt and paper, and hung across the door with string. "Macy *Mieko* MacHine."

"Yep," she answers, pushing her door open. "M.M.M."

"Wow," I say out loud. Her room is somehow the exact opposite of what I would've imagined it to be—all full of lightness and delicate colors (peaches and creams and the softest blues and tans)—yet at the same time, the more I get to know her, it also seems perfect.

She has a canopy over her bed, but instead of fabric it is covered with string and origami shapes stitched together in long strands that hang over the sides. It reminds me of this one Chrismukkah a few years ago when Noah and I stayed up late and attempted to make popcorn and dried cranberry garlands, except we ate most of it in the process, so they ended up being sad-looking strings. This origami garland looks as pretty as I thought our popcorn garland was going to be.

There are soft twinkle lights wrapped around the shades of two bedside lamps, and when she flips her light switch, they automatically light up, giving everything a soft, dreamy glow. As my eyes travel all around, they're drawn upward—a sky mural, painted blue and dotted with cotton candy-like clouds, covers the entire ceiling.

On Macy's bedside table I see a framed picture. It's of a younger Macy and a woman who looks a little bit like Macy and a little bit like her sobo too—Macy's mom.

"Macy, this is like a fairy bedroom—everything's so magical!"

She grins ear to ear. "You like it?"

"I love it. I mean, you have a sky!"

"That's my favorite part too," she says, looking upward. "They painted it like that when I was little."

"Who's 'they'?" I ask.

"My parents. Well, my mom mostly," but Macy quickly changes the subject, striding across her room, saying, "Oh! Sadie, here, come meet Dango."

I rush over to where she is standing. In the corner of her bedroom is a giant cage that seems big enough to hold a big dog, except it has two stories lined with shredded paper and aspen wood bedding, with miniature houses that look like they were built for gnomes, along with little tufts of hay scattered here and there. There's a half-eaten lettuce leaf and a celery stalk sticking out of a little food bowl filled with green bunny food pellets. I look all over, but I don't see the rabbit.

Macy opens a little door on the side of the cage and wiggles her fingers through the shredded papers, saying, "Hello, Dango? I'm home."

That's when I notice something familiar. On the wall, right outside of Dango's cage, is a piece of paper, taped at the corners, almost like it's a decoration for Dango's home. It's the origami bunny I drew for Macy.

And suddenly two bunny ears pop up from the roof of the gnome house, followed by a tiny high-pitched squeal. Dango hops—a blur of peach fur—toward Macy, in a way that reminds me of how a dog would greet their special human.

Macy picks Dango up and brings him to a soft rug in the middle of the room, where he stretches out to twice his original puffball size.

"He's so big and adorable!" I say as he barrels toward me and stands up on his hind legs to sniff me before he lets me pet him. "And soft!"

"The softest," Macy agrees, reaching over to scratch between Dango's ears.

"I pictured him as so much smaller, but he's the size of my cat!"

"He was so small when I first adopted him. When my grandma saw him for the first time, she said he looked like a little dumpling, except she said *dango*, 'dumpling' in Japanese," she explains. "So we just started calling him that!"

Macy's grandma comes in right then, carrying a big tray full of all kinds of snacks. Veggies and crackers and pickle spears, yogurt, and what look like little cookies or pastries.

"Thank you, Sobo," Macy says.

"Work hard, girls." As she leaves the room, we hear her say, "Don't play with Dango and ignore your schoolwork."

"We won't," Macy calls after her.

"You don't have to eat the veggies; Dango can help us—broccoli and green peppers are his favorite treat in the world." Macy whispers, and as she holds out a thin slice of pepper for Dango he grabs it with his tiny paws and starts gnawing on it. "But try one of the little cakes—they're so yummy."

I choose one of the balls of dough and take a bite. It's soft and sticky, with this sweet marshmallow texture on the inside, but floury like a cookie on the outside. "It's so delicious!" I exclaim.

"Mochi," she says. "My grandma makes them."

"Lucky you!" I say, even though my mouth is still full. But then I start thinking about Gramps and his epic PB&J sandwiches; I start to feel a little guilty for wanting to avoid him.

"What's wrong?" Macy asks. I guess she can tell from the look on my face that something is bothering me. "It's not the mochi, is it?"

"No," I tell her. "Just thinking about Gramps and your sobo and . . . family stuff." I look up at the sky-painted ceiling again.

"Here, let me show you something," Macy says, standing up. She walks over to the window and closes her curtains and turns off the ceiling light. And as she comes to sit next to me again the ceiling is slowly illuminated with glow in the dark stars, but not the stick-on kind like Jude had in her old bedroom. These are painted into constellations.

"Wow," I breathe. "Your mom did all this?"

Macy nods as we both admire the sky above us.

"It was almost two years ago," she says quietly. "When my mom died."

My heart plummets. "Macy . . ." I begin.

"It's okay." She tries to smile but she has tears in her eyes.

I don't really know what to say, but I try to find something.

"I'm so sorry, and I'm so, so sad for you."

Dango climbs up into Macy's lap, like he knows that she needs him.

"I know you said before that you didn't want to talk about it, but if you ever do, I'd like to hear about her."

"Thanks," she says. "I will want to someday. Just not today."

## Chapter 16

# MARSHMALLOW

The entire way home, my thoughts are divided between Macy and her family on one side and trying to prepare myself to face Gramps on the other.

"Gramps, I'm home!" I say, making my way toward the kitchen. I expect to find him in there, lining up all the PB&J ingredients.

I set my backpack down on the floor, and when I look through the window, I catch sight of the door of Mama's She Shed swinging wide open.

"What the . . . ?" I mutter to myself.

I race back into the living room and grab an umbrella from the metal holder we keep by the door. "Gramps?" I call once more.

No answer.

I try to channel the bravery of S. Hawkins and grip the handle of the umbrella tightly as I open the back door and follow the path of stones through the backyard, past the fairy fortress, toward the shed.

I hear sounds coming from inside, like things are being moved around. My first thought: It's an art thief, here to steal Mama's mosaics. They've done something with Gramps. Locked him in the trunk of a car or blindfolded him and set him loose in the woods to try to find his way back, but not before they had finished the heist—this is probably why my moms don't like me watching Noah's action movies.

"Hello?" I yell, my steps slowing down the closer I get.

More sounds: something being dragged, clicking, and footsteps. I keep my eyes wide open, watching closely, my umbrella at the ready. I stand on the other side of the door and inhale—*I'm brave,* I try to tell myself—and just as I take a step, I slam directly into someone.

I scream, gripping the handle of my umbrella so hard that I accidentally press the button that makes it pop open, and the person in front of me—who I can no longer see because of the rainbow of colors blocking my view—also screams.

"Sass!"

I fumble to move my umbrella, but then I can see that it's Gramps, eyes as wide as mine, a hand pressed to his chest.

"Gramps!" I yell back.

"Don't you know not to sneak up on old people?" he says, leaning over with both of his hands on his knees, breathing out a big *whooo* sound.

"Sorry, Gramps. I said hello first and you didn't answer!"

"Well, don't you know old people can't hear? At least *this* old person, anyhow."

I try to peek around him to see inside the shed.

"*What are you doing?*" we say to each other at the same time.

"Expecting rain?" he asks, gesturing at the umbrella now on the ground.

"I thought you might be a burglar." I pick up the umbrella and prop it up against the side of the shed. "Or something," I add.

"I see," he says, pulling the shed door closed behind him.

"So . . . what *are* you doing out here, Gramps?" I ask again.

Gramps presses his lips together like he's about to either smile or frown but hasn't decided which. "Here," he says, holding his arm out. "Let's take a walk, you and me. Walks are good for our health."

We follow the path that leads to the gate at the back of the yard. Gramps opens it and lets me go first, latching it closed behind us. When we get to the clearing, I think about how this was where I first saw Dewey.

As if he can read my mind, Gramps says, "I wanted to talk through this whole dog situation."

"Dewey, you mean. Right?" I ask, trying to get a sense of where Gramps's mind is today.

"Yes, Dewey," he repeats.

"Did I tell you this is where I first saw her?" I ask, twirling in a circle to take in the whole 360 degrees of the clearing. "I pulled one of those prickly burr thingies out of her paw, and I think that's when she chose me."

"Chose you?" Gramps asks. "How do you mean?"

"I don't know, really. Chose me to be her friend. To take care of her." And then I add, "Chose me to talk to."

He grins at me, and nods like he understands.

"It's a special thing to be chosen," he says.

We walk slowly down the trail that leads through the woods, both of us sort of quiet, but not in a bad way.

"Did your mom ever tell you about Marshmallow?" Gramps suddenly asks.

"Marshmallow?" I repeat, as if it was the first time I'd heard that name. "No. What's that?"

"*Who's* that," he corrects me. "Marshmallow was our dog that we had when your mom was a little girl. He was mostly your grandmother's dog, though—just don't ever tell your mom that."

"Really?" I ask, so excited because I don't hear many stories about Mom's mom. "What was he like? Marshmallow?" I repeat, loving the way his name is all sweet and cuddly.

"Oh, he was a little wiry thing, yappy, smelly, wouldn't do anything unless your mother—I mean your grandmother—was the one doing the asking." He pauses and laughs. "But loyal. He was the best dog. I remember he showed up on our doorstep during a storm one night, and he was so scrawny and hungry and dirty."

"What happened to him?"

"We never knew where he came from, but that night your grandmother said the same thing to me—that he *chose* us. And that meant we were obligated to give him a home. To love him. To keep him safe."

"And you kept him?"

"We did. And he was with us for the next twelve years. Marshmallow was the first animal your mom ever loved. She got that from your grandmother—wanting to help animals. And I think you've got it too, Sass."

"Mom doesn't ever talk about her—Grandma, I mean."

He nods, saying, "She misses her."

We walk a while longer and Gramps doesn't say much; he just looks off into the trees.

"I like hearing stories about her," I add.

Gramps looks at me then and smiles so bright and big. "I like telling them."

"It doesn't make you miss her too much?" I ask, thinking now not only of Mom but of Macy too, wondering if that's why she hasn't wanted to tell me too much about her mother.

"In a way, but . . ." He stops walking as we come to a clearing, and there's a little pond in the center. He sits down carefully on top of a fallen tree trunk and I hop up next to him while we watch the ripples in the water. "I'd rather remember her, even if it makes me miss her too. I suppose it makes me feel like she's not so far away when I tell stories about her."

"Makes sense," I say, but he's staring off, like he's looking far into the sky beyond the outline of trees way on the other side of the pond, and I'm not sure he heard me.

"Remember her while I can," he says quietly.

*While he can.*

"Gramps?"

I say his name in place of the question I don't know how to ask. Quiet stretches out between us, and I need to break up the silence.

"Are you disappointed in me? I mean, because I made up the story about the poster? Are you going to tell Moms?"

"I could never be disappointed in you, not when your heart is in the right place. Grown-ups don't know everything," he continues. "Sometimes it seems like the older we get, the more we forget to lead with our hearts. When your heart is in the right place, that's what really counts, isn't it?"

"I . . . I think so," I answer.

"I think so too," he agrees. "And I think your Dewey is a lot like our Marshmallow: deserving of a second chance."

"So you'll talk to Moms about it?" I ask, hearing the hope in my voice.

"You just leave it to me," he says, not fully answering my question.

I want to ask him what he means by that, but he's staring off into the distance like he's deep in thought again—maybe wandering into another memory—and so I just sit there next to him listening to the sounds of the wind in the leaves, the small scurrying footsteps of squirrels, and the birds calling back and forth to one another.

Gramps shakes his head slightly, breaking his concentration, and then he looks down at me and pats the log we're sitting on.

"You know, I like this spot," he says, looking around like it's only now that he's fully seeing the landscape surrounding us.

"I do too," I tell him, happy to have him back from wherever his mind had taken him. "Moms won't ever let me go into the woods by myself."

"They're right—but," he says excitedly, "you're not alone if you're with me."

I nod.

"We'll come back here," Gramps declares, standing up

from the log and brushing the dried crumbles of leaves off his pants. "But for now, we should be heading home, don't you think?"

We walk back in the direction we came.

Gramps stops when we reach the gate and says, "I want to show you something. In the—uhh—Her House."

"Do you mean the She Shed?"

"Right. She Shed." He leads the way, pushing the door open.

Inside, Mama's boxes of art supplies are all stacked up under her desk, and there is now a rug laid out in the center of the floor, and a brand-new fluffy dog bed in the corner. There is a basket full of bones, stuffed animals, and rubber toys. And two dog bowls laid out on a bone-shaped mat—one for water and one for food.

Gramps picks up one of the toys from the basket and squeaks it.

"Well, what do you think?" he asks.

I'm so stunned I can barely find words to respond. "Gramps, what—what is all this?"

"I like to call it the Puppy Palace."

"Does this mean . . ." I pause, feeling my heart getting light and fluttery. "We can really adopt Dewey?"

I want to say *thank you* and *oh my gosh* and *I can't believe it* and *you're amazing* and *am I dreaming?* but my mind is going so fast I can't catch one single thought long enough to actually form any words. I close my eyes, letting my mind take it all in.

Dewey will be saved!

"It might still need some finishing touches from you," he says. "But it's all decked out with everything she'll need. Heck, it's almost nicer than my room back in the main house, even!"

"But how—when—where did you get all of this stuff?"

"Where do you think, silly? The pet store."

As I look around at the new dog supplies all over Mama's art studio, Gramps's words sink into my mind a little deeper, and my heart, which was so full and hopeful only a minute ago, is now overtaken with a sick, heavy feeling. Because why are we setting up a space for Dewey out here instead of in the house? Unless . . .

"My moms don't know about this, do they?"

He lets out a small chuckle. "Well, we already know what they would say, don't we?"

"Yes," I answer. "They'd say no."

"So what's wrong?" he asks. "I thought you'd be happy?"

"It's just—how will this work? Moms will find out, and I don't know, I would want Dewey inside, as part of the family, not hiding out here."

And then there's the other part, the part that already has

my muscles getting all knotted up throughout my body. "We'd be keeping a secret from Moms," I tell him. "Lying."

"It's a temporary solution. We keep Dewey here until it's the right time to tell your moms, and in the meantime, she won't be alone. I'll be able to take care of her during the day when everyone's gone, and you'll have time to play with her and walk her after school," he explains. "It's better than the alternative, right?"

I nod reluctantly. I can't argue with that. "Anything is better than the alternative."

"Then don't worry!" he snaps at me, his voice turning loud and sharp for a moment. Then, softer, he continues, "Think of it as me wanting to give you, my granddaughter, a dog. I have every right to give you a gift, don't I?"

"I guess," I say. "I mean yes."

"That's right," he agrees, but then he shifts away from me slightly and mumbles, "Your mother can't take that away from me."

"What?"

"Nothing," he says. "I can still make some decisions for myself, you know."

"I know, Gramps."

"I know you know, Sass—you might be the only one who does. I don't mean to be getting grumpy with you. You know what; we'll talk more about this later."

## Chapter 17

# THE MOST IMPORTANT THING

Gramps never comes out of his room for dinner. My moms act like it isn't a big deal, but I can see the creased foreheads and frown lines in their faces as they look at each other across the table.

I start to worry he might be upset with me for not being as enthusiastic as he had hoped I'd be about the whole Puppy Palace thing.

After dinner I go to my room to find a series of messages waiting for me on my laptop.

JUDE: check your phone! I called a bunch of times. . . .

JUDE: I am sooo sorry I forgot to call you back the other day!!!

JUDE: pls call as soon as you can

JUDE: I want to hear abt your butterflyer

It took her two whole days to realize she forgot about my emergency. Checking my phone, I see that she called three times in a row while I was eating dinner. I close my bedroom door and sit on my bed, taking a deep breath before calling back.

"Sadie!" she shouts into the phone.

"Hi."

"Sade, I'm so, so, so sorry."

"It's okay," I lie.

"So what is it? What's the butterflyer about?" she asks, and if I close my eyes tight, I can almost imagine that she's here sitting across from me. "It's not about Gramps, is it?"

"Well," I begin. "It wasn't before, but now it might be . . ."

I tell her everything, starting at the beginning: meeting Dewey in the woods, then again at the shelter; the poster with Macy's number; and Gramps and the Puppy Palace, and finish with the fact that now I have no idea what to do next.

"Wait, your archenemy Macy? Mean Machine Macy, who has never spoken to—never been nice to—anyone *ever*, who you have been avoiding all year, *that* Macy is helping you?"

"That's what you're most surprised about! What about the dog part?"

"I guess a telepathic dog is more believable than a nice Macy."

Jude snickers, but I don't.

"Macy is a lot different than we thought, Jude," I say. Jude is silent for a few seconds, so I keep talking. "She's sort of the only friend I have here now."

"Ohh-kaaay." Jude says, slowly, and I can't tell what the pointy edges of those two syllables mean.

"Jude?"

"Jeez, sorry," she finally says. "I didn't know."

"No, it's okay. It's just that—" I stammer, but I'm not sure what I'm really even trying to say. "The point is, what am I supposed to do now?"

It's so quiet on the line, I can hear Jude's breathing.

"This is the butterflyer part I need you for," I say.

Jude makes this weird noise, like there's something stuck in her throat.

"What?"

"Nothing. It's just—I wouldn't exactly call this a butter-flyer."

My heart starts beating fast, like there might just be butterfly wings flapping in my chest, sending jolts of electricity down my arms and legs. "How is this *not* a butter-flyer?" I hear it in my voice, all sharp and tense, just like Gramps's was earlier.

"*Talking dogs?*" she says, a giggle lurking behind the words.

"You're making it sound stupid—it's not that simple."

"Okay, sorry!" she says.

Her words hang there, and the silence stretches out like taffy, until it seems like too much space has come between us and there are no more words left to say to her. She doesn't understand. Why doesn't she understand?

And then finally, she does laugh. Like it's a joke.

"I have to go," I say it quick, and then I hang up without even waiting for her to respond.

I throw my phone on my bed as hard as I can—it bounces off the pillow and lands with a soft thud on top of the comforter. Any other time I've been this angry with someone, I talk to Jude about it and that makes me feel better. Except this time it's Jude I'm angry with—and what's worse is that I still don't have any advice on what I'm supposed to do!

I grab my pillow with both hands, smash my face into it, open my mouth, and *scream* at the top of my lungs. When I pull my face away, I'm out of breath and my eyes are watering.

My gaze settles on my graphic novel on the nightstand, and I really wish that I could time travel like S. Hawkins. I'd go back to the morning I met Dewey and just get her to the house, before she got taken to the shelter. Then she'd be here right now, and I wouldn't be fighting with Jude, and Gramps wouldn't be coming up with this plan that seems bound to backfire on us.

**It's impossible to** sleep. My conscience is keeping me awake. I haven't even agreed to take part in Gramps's idea about keeping Dewey in the Puppy Palace, and I already feel like I'm guilty.

"Dewey?" I whisper into the darkness of my bedroom. "I promise I'm still trying."

*I'm still waiting.*

There's got to be a better way.

I jump out of bed. I know what I need to do: I'm going to tell my moms everything. Maybe the honesty will work in my favor. Besides, they should know about all the little things that have been happening when I'm with Gramps, the way it seems like he's getting more and more confused. And who knows, I think, maybe if they hear what Gramps is planning, they'll understand how important Dewey is to me—to both of us—and they'll figure out a way to make it work for us to adopt her.

I creep across the hall to their bedroom, and as I peek inside, I see that the two lights on each of their nightstands are on. They are talking quietly, so I stand outside their door for a second to make sure I'm not interrupting. I raise my hand to knock, take a deep breath, and just as my knuckles graze the surface of the door, I hear Mom say something that freezes me where I stand.

"A nursing home, Elle, really?" Mom sniffles. "How did we get here so quickly?"

"Love, it's not a nursing home. It's assisted living," Mama says. "There's a difference."

"Not to him, there's not." Mom lets her head fall into her hand, and she takes in a shaky gasp of air. There are brochures spread out across their bed.

Mama picks another one up and unfolds it, showing it to Mom. "Look at this one, Katie. Oakwood Village. It has a pond. Art classes. It's only twenty-five minutes away. He could still be very independent, but also get the help he needs."

"I'm not ready to do this," Mom says. "Can we just wait a little while longer? Maybe"—Mom's voice cracks—"he'll get settled in once he's done being angry with me. Maybe we'll all find a good rhythm and things will balance out?"

Mama puts her arm around Mom's shoulder and pulls her closer, whispering, "Maybe."

Mom leans into her, pushing the blanket of brochures to the floor as she lies down. I've never seen her like this.

Usually Mom is the one who knows what to do, always the one to comfort everyone else, never letting the murky feelings get to her—at least, that's what I thought, anyway. There's no way I'm going to tell them about Gramps now, for his sake and for theirs. It would just cause more sadness.

I go downstairs, expecting to find Gramps having his usual midnight snack. He's not there. So I walk down the hall to his room. Not there either. The bed is made and he has some books lined up on the desk, along with his pad of sketch paper and drawing pencils. I shouldn't snoop, I know. But I take a few steps into the bedroom to see what Gramps is working on. He has a small picture of my grandmother in a frame that is propped up against the wall. In it, her mouth is just a little bit blurred—she must've been in the middle of saying something. In her lap sits a small, scruffy-looking dog.

I look down at the paper and see that he had been sketching her face, except he's making it life-sized. And unlike a lot of Gramps's drawings that are cartoony, this one is so realistic I feel like her face might come to life right out of the paper. Her eyes are the part that is most complete. The rest of her face is still swashes and light marks of an outline.

Gramps is the one who taught me to start with the eyes,

but when I look into hers, they feel so real and warm, and I wonder if Gramps is focusing on them not just because that's the way he draws. I compare the drawing with the photo. There's something about the drawing that feels more real—like I can sense her personality, can even imagine the sound of her voice.

I carefully pick up the picture frame and look closer at my grandmother's face. She's so happy, surrounded by flowers all around her and the dog; she even holds a stem between her fingers. And she's young too—probably younger than my mom is now. I can see why Gramps always says that Mom reminds him of her. I never saw it before now, but in this picture, Mom has Grandma's exact smile.

Although, I haven't seen Mom laugh like this in a long time.

"I wish you were still here," I whisper, the words cloudy and shaky. I try to set the picture back down in exactly the same spot I found it in.

I walk back through the living room and into the kitchen—there are only so many places he could be. It's so dark out I can barely see the outline of the She Shed/Puppy Palace, but then I spot Gramps sitting outside on the back porch, looking out at the trees.

He doesn't notice me there as I open the door. "Gramps?" I ask quietly.

"Hmm?" he answers, still looking into the distance.

"Gramps, what are you doing outside in the dark?"

"Just looking at the stars," he says, sounding sleepy. There's a sadness coming from him—just like there's a sadness coming from Mom upstairs. But that sadness wasn't there earlier when he was showing me all the things he bought for Dewey. He was excited then. He was doing something that made him feel good. Something from his heart—and that is the most important thing, like he said. Why would I want to take that from him?

"Gramps, if we were going to go through with this plan, how would it work?"

He looks up at me and smiles.

## Part Three

# CODE NAME: HOME, SWEET HOME

## Chapter 18

# THE SLEEPOVER

Six o'clock, Friday night, the doorbell rings.

Macy and I spent all day in school going over the plan: how she'd spend the night, so we could all get to the shelter early in the day; how Gramps was in charge of coming up with a way to get Moms out of the house tomorrow.

Mama goes to answer the door, and Gramps and I share a look across the dinner table. The plan is now officially in action.

Mama invites Macy and her dad inside, and they shake hands, exchanging first names the way grown-ups always do. If I could see bits of Macy's grandma in Macy before, now I can see that she has some of her dad too. His hair is curly just like Macy's, except his is bright red instead of brown, but he has the same dusting of freckles across his nose and cheeks.

"I've heard so much about you," Mama says. "I'm so glad you could come over."

"Thanks for having her," Macy's dad says.

"You're welcome to come in and stay for dinner too—my wife's bringing home a pizza."

He looks at his watch. "Thank you, but I should be getting back to Macy's grandmother."

Mama nods, and says quietly, "We have a grandparent here too."

On cue, Gramps is there in the doorway, shaking Macy's dad's hand, saying, "I'm Grandpa Ed. Gramps for short." Then he says, "And you must be the famous Origami Macy I've heard so much about. I am pleased to finally make your acquaintance—you're a very talented young person."

This makes her cheeks turn all flushed, and she looks down at her feet. "Thank you. Nice to meet you too."

"Have fun," Macy's dad says, giving her a quick hug before he leaves.

As Macy walks into my room, she looks all around at my things—my books and art supplies and collection of stuffed animals—and I hope she's not going to think I'm a baby for still having so many toys everywhere. She doesn't say anything, though, until she reaches my desk. She taps her finger against the origami rabbit she gave me.

"You kept it," she finally says.

"Of course I did," I tell her. "That's why Gramps calls you Origami Macy."

"I like that better than my other nickname." Macy

grimaces. Before I can say anything to try to make her feel better, her eyes light up. "That's her, isn't it!" Macy exclaims. She's standing in front of my drawing of Dewey hanging on the wall. "I can't wait to see her in real life."

"I can't wait to see her again either," I tell her.

There's a *bloopbloop* sound coming from my desk.

"What's that?" Macy asks.

I walk over and close my laptop. "It's Jude. Video call."

"You can answer if you want."

"No, it's okay." I shrug, like me not wanting to talk to Jude is no big deal. "I can call her back later."

"Oh." Macy's voice is barely a whisper. "Is it because you don't want her to know that we're friends now?"

"What? No, of course not! Besides, she knows that we're friends already anyway."

"Really?" Macy's eyes light up. "And she doesn't think you shouldn't be hanging out with me?"

"Well, maybe she was surprised at first because we thought that you hated me," I begin, but I can't tell her the whole truth because that would just hurt her feelings.

Outside, I hear a car door shut. Once. And twice. A scuffle of shoes and bags and jingling keys as Mom and Noah come through the door.

"*Honey, I'm ho-ome!*" Noah bellows, copying something he saw on TV that's supposed to be funny but isn't.

"Hey, guys, we got some pizza—including a very

special veggie deluxe for you, my dear," I hear Mom say, so much more cheerful than she was last night in her bedroom when she didn't know I was listening.

Noah bounds up the stairs, stopping in my doorway. "Oh look, Dweeb One and Dweeb Two," he says, tromping past us. "Dinner's here."

"My brother," I explain to Macy. "He's clueless."

He makes a fart sound with his mouth and disappears down the hall into his bedroom.

"Hi, Macy." Mom waves as we enter the kitchen. "I'm the other mom."

As we all sit down at the table, Mama pours herself and Mom each a glass of wine and asks, "So, how was everyone's day? Anything exciting happen?"

"No," Gramps and I say at the same time.

Macy shakes her head so vigorously I'm afraid it's going to look suspicious, but Mom takes a sip from her glass and doesn't seem to notice.

"Nothing exciting happened with me either, and I'll tell you what, I am fine with that," Mama continues. "I'm so ready for the weekend."

"Hear, hear," Mom says, raising her glass, which Mama clinks against hers.

Noah swipes a slice of pizza from the box and starts to dash out of the kitchen.

"Hey, mister," Mom says, tugging on Noah's shirtsleeve. "What, do we have cooties? Why don't you sit down and join us a minute?"

"I already ate at Kendra's," he mumbles, mouth full of pizza.

"*His girlfriend,*" I whisper to Macy.

"Sit down, Noah," Mama agrees. "When is the last time we were all home on a Friday night and not having to get something done or be somewhere?"

Mom's eyes crinkle at the edges, and a mischievous smirk slowly takes shape on her lips. "You know what I think this calls for?"

Noah and I share a look—we know what she means.

Noah groans, but I shout, "Yay!"

"What?" Gramps looks at Mom, waiting. "What does this call for?"

Mom rubs her hands together, and then in her goofy voice she finally answers, "Board game night." She says it that way, like a challenge, because she is *very* competitive when it comes to board games—she's definitely not one of those parents who lets the kids win just because they're kids.

"Oh, I don't know, Katie," Gramps says. "I'm still recovering from the great Parcheesi incident of 1987." Which makes both Mom and Mama crack up.

Noah leans toward me and says under his breath, "Do we even want to know what they're talking about?"

"Probably not," I answer, recognizing that this is the first time in forever that he's speaking to me in a way that is just *normal* and not mean.

Macy and I go to the closet in the hall where my family keeps our games, and we bring as many game boxes back to the table as we can carry.

While we roll the dice and draw the cards and keep score of our points, it feels like old times, when we used to visit Gramps at his apartment and just hang out, being a family. I don't even mind that we're having pizza yet again. The only thing that could make this family night more perfect is if Dewey were here already, sleeping at my feet.

It's only when Catniss decides to jump up onto the table and swipe at the game pieces on the board that Mama stretches in her chair and looks at the time on the microwave.

"Eleven o'clock!" she exclaims. "I think we should call it a night, guys."

"You mean you forfeit," Mom says.

"Yes," Mama giggles. "We bow down to you, oh queen of all board games."

We begin putting all the games back in their boxes, and

Mom says she's heading up to bed. "We have a big day tomorrow, don't we, Dad?"

Gramps looks at me, catching my wide-eyed worried expression. *Tomorrow?* I mouth.

"How's that, Katie?" he asks Mom. "What's happening tomorrow?"

"Dad, you asked me just this afternoon if we could go by your apartment to pack some of your things up so you have them here."

"Oh, that," Gramps says. "Yes. Of course I remember—I just didn't think that qualifies as a big day."

"Girls, say good night to Gramps, all right?" Mama says. "And brush your teeth before bed."

When Gramps hugs me, he whispers, "*Close call,*" and winks, which tells me two things: one, he knows exactly what's going on, and two, he came through on his plan to get Moms out of the house tomorrow in a very believable way.

**Upstairs in my** bedroom, Moms have laid out an air mattress.

"I had a lot of fun tonight," Macy says as she lies down in my bed.

"Me too." And it's true; I did. But as we get settled in

and turn the lights off, my mind starts to go through all of the possible things that could go wrong with Code Name: Home, Sweet Home.

"Macy?" I begin. "Are you still awake?"

"Mm-hmm."

I sit up on the air mattress so we're at eye level. "There's something I should tell you about Dewey." I pause, trying to figure out the least strange way to say it. She turns over on her side so that she can face me. "Have you ever felt like you knew what Dango was thinking?"

"Sure."

"Not from the way he acts, but like . . . he talks to you."

"What?" Her eyebrows knit together as she looks at me with confusion. "Like, out loud?"

"No, not out loud, but like that his thoughts are in your head. Telepathy, I mean."

"No," she answers slowly. "Why?"

"Well, it's sort of like that with Dewey and me."

Macy props herself up on her elbow now, narrowing her eyes at me. "Are you serious?"

I cringe, not wanting her to think I'm crazy. I nod instead of answering out loud.

"Stop," she says, giggling. "You're just trying to see if I'm that gullible!"

"It's the truth," I tell her. "I mean, or maybe I'm just imagining it."

"Wait, you're not joking?" she says, her face smoothing out into something like a grin. "This explains how you knew so much about her!"

"It feels so good to have the truth out, finally! Gramps is the only other person who knows. And Jude," I add, "but I'm pretty sure she doesn't believe me."

"Well, I do."

We lie back down, and I feel light and floaty, like a feather.

"Sadie," Macy says. "Do you know why people started calling me Mean Machine?"

I remember it was after she got into those fights with the older kids when we were in third grade. I'm a little confused about why she's bringing this up now, but I answer, "Yes, I—I think so."

"I'm not sure you do," she tells me.

I sit up again so I can see her.

"Those older kids," she continues. "They had somehow found out that my mom had just died and that my sobo had moved in with us, and they started saying mean things to me—bullying me, making fun of me for not having a mom."

"What?" I gasp.

"And I couldn't think of any words to say back because I was so sad and so angry. So I punched them." She rubs her eyes. "I know it's not right to ever hit anyone, but—"

"I would've done the same thing," I interrupt, feeling so many lava-like emotions boiling up inside of me.

She turns her head to look at me, and even though she's crying, she smiles. "So that's the real story."

"It was so wrong of them to do that, Macy! I can't believe anyone would be so cruel."

She nods, and continues, "The principal said I could stay in school and not be expelled for fighting if my dad made sure I went to counseling—to, you know, talk about my feelings about my mom and everything."

"And that's where you go on Thursday mornings," I realize, all the pieces finally coming together.

"It helps," she says. "Sometimes."

"If I'd have known what really happened, I promise I would've tried to be your friend before."

"Thanks, Sadie." She yawns, and murmurs, "I'm just glad we're friends now."

"So am I," I tell her, but I think she's already asleep.

I try to fall asleep too, but I toss and turn. I look at my alarm clock. Almost midnight. I wonder if Dewey's sleeping right now, if she knows that tomorrow we'll be coming for her. I look at Dewey's picture on my wall and focus hard, shut my eyes tightly, and tell her, *Soon, Dewey, I'll be there soon.*

## Chapter 19

# D-DAY (D FOR DEWEY)

Eight thirty a.m., Saturday. Rubbery store-bought doughnuts for breakfast. No French toast, but I can't complain
because today is the day.

I still eat half of a white-powdered doughnut and half
of a waxy-chocolate-covered one. Macy goes for a chocolate. Gramps takes one of the plain doughnuts and frowns
while he dunks it in his coffee.

"Dad?" Mom asks Gramps. "You all right?"

"You tell me," he answers, sulking. "Apparently I'm not
'all right' enough to pack up my own belongings."

Gramps winks at Macy and me—this is part of his plan
to get Moms out of the house.

"Ed, you understand," Mama interjects. "With all the
lifting and sorting and going up and down the stairs. You
don't want to do all that anyway, do you?"

"When you put it like that, it does sound like pretty

hard labor." Gramps shifts his eyes over to Noah, who is stuffing his face with alternating bites of white-powdered, cinnamon-covered, and chocolate doughnuts. "Nothing a strapping youngster like yourself can't handle, though. Right?"

"Who, me?" Noah mumbles, powdered sugar coating the corners of his lips. "Do I have to?" Noah whines.

Mama collects our doughnut plates, messing Noah's hair with her free hand on her way to the sink. "No, you don't *have* to, Noah . . ."

"But it would be nice if you offered," Mom finishes. She stands and starts clearing hers and Mama's empty coffee and tea mugs.

Noah sighs. Gramps holds his hand up and says, "Forget I said anything. Really, it's okay. Don't want to overstep my place. After all, I'm *just* the grandpa."

After their backs are turned, Gramps silently slips his wallet out of his pocket and pulls out a crisp twenty-dollar bill, waving it at Noah and tipping his head as if to ask a silent question. Noah responds with an enthusiastic head nod that makes his hair bounce up and down. Gramps smiles and slides the twenty across the table.

Noah folds it up in his palm and announces, as he stands from his seat, "Actually, Moms, I'll come. I want to help."

"Really?" Mom asks, her eyebrows raised doubtfully.

"Yeah," Noah responds. "You're right, I should've offered to begin with."

Ten minutes later, after an elaborate conversation about the pros and cons of taking both cars (in which they decided they could fit more of Gramps's stuff if they took both), Mom, Mama, and Noah are finally ready to leave.

As they say their goodbyes, Mama pulls me aside. "Sadie, listen," she whispers as she threads her arms through her coat sleeves, "I want you to keep an eye on Gramps today, all right? If he starts acting strange, promise to call us right away." She leans over to kiss my forehead. "Okay?"

I look over my shoulder at Gramps. "Okay, Mama."

And they leave, at last. No one moves a muscle until we hear the cars pull out of the driveway. Then Gramps has his phone out, and mutters to himself. Macy and I stand near the door, impatiently waiting as we watch Gramps bring the phone closer to his face then farther away, tilting the screen this way and that, putting his glasses on and then taking them off, trying to see better.

Finally, he announces, "Our chariot is on its way, girls!"

"He means our Ryde," I tell Macy.

Armed with our checklist of rescue items, the three of us stand at the bottom of the driveway, waiting for a teal four-door sedan to pick us up. We huddle over Gramps's phone, watching the tiny car icon move across the map of streets to get to our house.

Macy and I slide into the back seat, and Gramps sits in the front. He talks with the driver the entire twelve minutes it takes to get to the animal shelter.

Seeing him here making conversation with this stranger, just like he used to talk with anyone in the park near his apartment, reminds me of the old Gramps. He is still who he has always been—the same friendly, fun-loving jokester.

Moms are wrong. He doesn't belong in some place for old people. He belongs with us.


**We walk toward** the entrance, and already I feel a huge rush of excitement flow through me like electricity. *Dewey*, I say in my thoughts, *I'm here!*

There are three people ahead of us in line at the reception desk. I decide to go wander and look at the cats so I don't draw any attention of someone who might recognize me. I stick my fingers into the cage of two gray tabby kittens, and they both try to grab my whole hand through the bars.

I'm giggling at them when I feel a tap on my shoulder, and a voice that's only a little familiar says, "Hey, Sadie!"

I turn around, and I'm relieved when I see who it is. "Patrick, hi!"

"Did you come in with your mom today?" Under his breath, Patrick adds, "You're not here for more Doodie Duty, are you?"

"No, not today—thankfully! I just came with my friend to pick up her lost dog." I hope I sound convincing even though my voice is shaky, as I point in the direction of Macy and Gramps standing in line at the reception desk. "Besides, Mom's not here today anyway," I correct.

"Ni-iii-ice . . ." Patrick says, smiling at Macy and Gramps. Then, as he looks back at me, he draws his eyebrows together like he's confused, hitching his thumb toward the offices behind us. "But I just saw your mom in the back."

"*What!*" I shout. "But . . . but she's not supposed to work on Saturdays."

"One of our other doctors was sick today. She must've gotten called in. What—why, what's wrong?"

"Nothing. Just. Can you please not mention to her that you saw me here? I'd be in really big trouble," I whisper.

He makes like he's zipping his lips and then tosses an invisible key over his shoulder. "I don't even see you right now. Who's talking to me?" he says, looking all around. "Guess I'm just talking to myself again. Get back to work, Patrick!" he mutters, walking away.

And immediately, I hear a familiar voice coming from down the hall. "Goodbye, little Miss Gracie. No more eating your dad's socks, okay, little girl?"

I peek my head around the corner and I freeze.

There's a man standing there with a short-legged, long-eared basset hound. But that's not the part that has my feet glued to the floor. It's the woman in the white coat leaning over to scratch under Gracie's floppy ears.

She stands up and hands the man a white paper bag and says, "She should be fine in a few days. Just be sure to give her this medicine twice a day with food."

"Thank you so much, Doctor."

It's. *Mom.*

And she's about to turn right toward me!

I force my feet to fly into action and whip back around the corner, plastering my body against the kitten crates. Underneath the frantic meowing of the two tabbies, I can hear Mom's footsteps coming down the hall. Closer and closer. I squeeze my eyes shut tight and pull my hood up over my head and hold my breath. I wait for her to find me.

But . . .

Hold on.

Her footsteps keep going.

I open one eye and turn my head just enough to see

her disappear into the back room. The door swings back and forth behind her with a *schwoopschwoop*.

I rush over to Gramps and Macy.

"*Mayday*," I whisper. "I repeat, *Mayday*. Mom. Is. Here!"

"What do you mean?" Gramps asks. "She's supposed to be at my apartment!"

"Oh no," Macy mumbles with her hand over her mouth. "No, no, no, no."

"Whaddowedo? Whaddowedo?"

Gramps looks worried, his eyes darting back and forth between Macy and me. "Sassafras, it's going to be okay, I promise." He steps forward in line. "Look, it's almost our turn."

But then I hear Mom's voice again, behind us. "Hey, you!" she coos. "What are you doing here?"

Macy grabs my hand and squeezes.

My heart turns to butterflies.

Gramps's eyes go wide.

I'm about to turn around and confess to everything. But then I hear a different voice answer, "Doc, Henry is having trouble with his back legs again."

"Oh, Henry," Mom's voice says, "what are we gonna do with you?"

"I didn't think you'd be here today, Dr. Mitchell-Rosen,"

Henry's owner says to Mom. "We have an appointment with Dr. Potter."

"I'm covering for Dr. Potter today, so you'll be with me." I hear Henry panting and whimpering excitedly. "Once you get checked in, we'll see what we can do about those back legs, Henry."

Then Mom's footsteps again, moving right alongside us.

Gramps turns in a circle as Mom walks by so that his back is facing her the whole time. She's behind the reception desk now, asking another person for Henry's file.

The person in front of us in line walks away.

We're up.

"Can I help you?" the receptionist asks Gramps—her name tag says MOLLY.

He rests his elbow on the counter and brings his hand up to his face like he's shielding his eyes from the sun. "Uhh, yes," he whispers.

There's no way Mom won't see us now!

"Pardon me?" Molly says, way too loudly.

Gramps clears his throat. Then holds up his finger, like *hold on*, turns away from the desk, and fake-coughs into his hand. He mouths the word *poster*, and Macy shoves the lost and found flyer into his hand. He turns back around and holds the flyer up so the receptionist can see, and whispers again, as quietly as possible, "We're here to pick up our dog."

"*What?*" she shouts again, drawing even more attention to us.

Mom turns around while skimming through the file folder in her hands.

Gramps sweeps the poster to the floor and ducks behind the desk.

"Sir?"

Macy bends over like she's tying her shoe.

I kneel to "help" Gramps pick up the paper.

I hear Mom say thank you to someone, and I pull the drawstrings on my hoodie tight so that it closes in on my face while I rise up slowly to peek over the desk.

"*She's coming!*" I whisper.

We all duck again.

More footsteps.

"Okay, Henry," Mom says, "right this way."

We all pop up from behind the desk, and Molly is looking at us with her face all scrunchy and contorted like we're the strangest people she's ever encountered. "Are you all okay?" she asks.

Gramps clears his throat and, all composed again, says, "Oopsie," and continues like nothing happened. "As I said, we're here to pick up my granddaughter's lost dog." Gramps pats the top of Macy's head and then hands over the flyer. "We got a call that she was brought in earlier this week. Her name's Dewdrop—"

"*Dewey!*" I whisper, nudging him with my elbow.

"Err, uh—uh, Dewey, I mean! Dewey," he stammers.

"For short," Macy adds. "We missed her so much."

Molly mutters, "All right, let's see here," as she types something and studies her computer screen. "Great, I'll have one of our techs bring her out in just a few minutes. Do you have her collar?"

Without speaking, I pull out the collar Gramps bought from my sweatshirt pocket, hand it to Macy, and then Macy hands it to Molly. Molly's eyes meet mine for a second too long, then her eyebrows pull together. "Hey," she says, "aren't you Dr. Mitchell-Rosen's kid?"

I shrug and shake my head, wordless, like one of those mimes I've seen on TV who look like clowns pretending they're inside of invisible boxes and stuff like that.

Macy jumps in and says, "No, this is my cousin. Her name's, uh—"

"Her name's Macy!" Gramps says, just as I'm spitting out "*Jude!*"

"Yeah," Macy says. "My cousin, Jud-cy? Ju-Judy, I mean. Judy."

"From out of town," Gramps adds.

"Salt Lake City," I tell her in my weird spur-of-the-moment version of a cowboy-type drawl to disguise my real voice.

Macy adds, "That's in Utah."

"*Allrightythen*," Molly says, shaking the thoughts of me out of her head. "Never mind, then."

"But back to Dewey, the reason we're here," Macy insists, redirecting the conversation. "We'll be sure to never let her out into the yard without her collar again, that's for sure! So, can we just go back and get her now?"

"I'll ask you to take a seat in the waiting area for now. It shouldn't be too long. We'll just need the fee, to cover the expenses of boarding Dewey this week."

"Oh, of course," Gramps says, pulling out his wallet.

Molly side-eyes us as we make our way over to the waiting area and find three seats next to each other. We don't dare speak until we're out of earshot.

"In the homestretch now," Gramps says.

"You saved us, Macy!"

"Quick thinking on your toes, girls," Gramps agrees.

"You too, Gramps! The way you ducked!" I giggle nervously, and Macy and Gramps join in.

*Sadie! Sadie! You came for me!*

I can hear Dewey calling me—I can feel how excited she is—I hear her barking, but it's different than her sad, lonely howl from the day we met.

"She's close," I whisper. "Dewey!" I yell out loud. And just as I do, I hear paws scrambling against the floor, struggling to go faster. Then, I see her. Rounding the corner, dragging a vet tech behind her, pulling so hard they stumble and drop Dewey's leash.

She runs toward me and I run toward her.

I kneel on the floor and she leaps up to put her paws on my shoulders, sniffing me all over and kissing my face, and I'm laughing so hard because I'm. Just. So. Happy.

*You came back! You came back! You came back!*

"I promised you I would!" I tell her, then look to Gramps and Macy who are beaming as they each take turns petting Dewey.

*You came back!*

Her tail is wagging back and forth, knocking into walls and chairs so hard I'm afraid she's going to hurt it.

"All right," Gramps says under his breath. "Let's blow this pupsicle stand, kids." He hitches his thumb in the direction of the reception desk where Molly is still watching us suspiciously.

## Chapter 20

# FREEDOM RIDE

Outside, I lead Dewey across the parking lot toward the teal four-door sedan. Macy and Gramps follow behind us. But as soon as I get to the door, I hear a click, and when I pull the handle, the door is locked. Gramps and Macy each try their doors too, and none of them budge.

That's when I see our Ryde driver's face. She's staring wide-eyed at Dewey, who's giving her the sweetest puppy dog face ever! *She's afraid,* Dewey tells me.

"No, there's nothing to be afraid of!" I shout through the window.

Dewey jumps up on the car door, so that she's face-to-face with the driver, and then she licks the glass. *Don't be afraid, I won't hurt you.*

But since it seems I'm the only one who can hear Dewey, the driver gets the wrong idea, and shrieks. Even more scared now, she fumbles with the car keys as she starts up the engine. Gramps knocks gently on her window, and all of us are shouting, "It's okay!"

She shakes her head, and just keeps repeating, "I can't, I'm sorry!" And then she reverses out of the parking spot.

"Wait! Don't go!" I shout. But it's too late.

She's gone.

Dewey pants nervously, looking all around.

And just then, there's a lawn mower–like rumble mixed with a high-pitched squealing coming from behind us. We each turn around, and almost in slow motion, like something out of an action movie, an old rusty car pulls out from behind the building. It glides up next to us, and the front window rolls down.

The driver lowers their sunglasses and says, "It looks like you could use a lift?"

"Patrick!" I shout. "Yes, we could—we really could!"

"Hop in," he says, reaching to unlock the back-seat and passenger-side doors.

Gramps and Macy look at Patrick uncertainly, then at me, and I know what they're thinking before they even have to ask.

"Don't worry, Patrick's a friend," I say. "We can trust him, I promise."

"Good enough!" Gramps replies, and gets into the front seat next to Patrick. "Name's Ed, the grandpa. Nice to meet you, Pat."

"Likewise," Patrick says, holding his hand for a fist bump.

Gramps awkwardly tries to shake Patrick's fist. In turn, Patrick switches to an open-palm high five position, which Gramps proceeds to bump with his fist. Macy and I get ourselves buckled into the back seat, Dewey sitting in between us.

"Gramps, we can teach you about fist bumps later. Step on it, Patrick!" I yell. And with a rumble of thunder from the engine, we squeal out of the parking lot and onto the road, the animal shelter growing smaller and smaller in the distance.

*You did it!* Dewey says, nuzzling her soft head under my chin. *You saved me!*

From the front seat, Patrick lowers all the windows, letting the cool air flow in.

"It's your freedom ride, Dewey!" Patrick shouts. *"Woooot!"*

We all cheer and *woot* and holler *yay* out the windows, Dewey chiming in with her own low, joyous baying like a wolf at the moon.


**On the drive** home, we fill Patrick in on everything about Code Name: Home, Sweet Home—except for the part about Dewey's telepathy.

He lets out a long exhale and glances over his shoulder

at me and Dewey in the back seat, and finally says, "I'm just glad I was there—you know I wasn't supposed to even be there today. I usually only work afternoons, but someone asked me to switch shifts with them at the very last minute today."

"Well," Gramps says, right as we're pulling into our driveway. "If there were ever a more fitting stroke of serendipity . . ." He doesn't finish his sentence, though; he just chuckles.

Macy and I look at one another with scrunched faces. "A stroke of what?" I finally ask.

"Serendipity," Gramps repeats. "It's when—well, it's hard to describe—it's when a little bit of luck and a little bit of magic come together at just the right time."

"Serendipity," I repeat to myself, the word making my mouth turn up into a smile.

## Chapter 21

# HOME, SWEET HOME

*We're home,* I silently tell Dewey. She follows us to the front door, but just before we walk through, there's a tug on her leash. She's looking into the house, her nose twitching and her tail trembling.

"What's wrong?" I ask, kneeling down next to her so I can see what's making her so afraid. "You're home."

*I'm not afraid, really. Just nervous. I've never been home before. What if I'm not any good at it?*

"You'll be great at it, you'll see. You belong here, I promise. Come on, I'll show you."

Gramps then appears in the doorway behind Macy and calls out to us, "Home, sweet home, Dewey!"

With that, she finally comes inside, but she sticks next to me like glue as we show her around the living room and the kitchen. Gramps fills a bowl with water and sets it on the floor next to Catniss's bowls. Dewey takes a bite of Catniss's cat food and then fills up on fresh water.

The whole time she's jumping from one spot to the next, sniffing everything, saying, *What's this? And this? Oh, what's this? That's new. That's weird. I like that. I don't know what that is. So many smells!*

I spot Catniss lurking way on top of the kitchen cabinets, hiding behind the big pot that doesn't fit into the cupboard where we keep the rest of the pots and pans. It's the one Moms pull out at Halloween and fill with candy for trick-or-treaters because they say it's like a witch's cauldron. Catniss is up there watching our every move. It's probably a good thing that Dewey doesn't see her yet.

But as soon as I think it, Dewey looks up above the cabinets.

Catniss ducks behind the cauldron. I wish I could tell what *she's* thinking right now. I hope she isn't able to somehow tell Noah there's been a dog in the house.

Dewey follows her nose all the way upstairs and goes directly to my bedroom. It's only then that she starts to relax. Her tail wag slows down and she begins sniffing things at a slower pace. I sit down on my bed, and Dewey jumps up next to me.

She sniffs at the pillow and blankets and then looks up at me, her eyes all bright and hopeful. *This is where we sleep?*

"Well . . . not exactly." My heart sinks a little, and she can tell something is wrong. Her ears twitch and lie flat against her head as I explain the whole situation—how we have to keep her being here a secret from my moms. She listens to everything, eyes wide and unblinking, paying such close attention, so she doesn't miss anything.

*I don't sleep here with you?*

"No, but we have a special house set up for you with a nice warm bed and toys and food and water and everything you need. It's your very own Puppy Palace!"

She blinks at me, unimpressed.

I give her a hug to try to cheer her up.

"It's so much better than where you were before. And besides. It's only for now. Until I can prove to Moms that I'm responsible, and then, somehow, we'll figure out how to tell them, and they'll understand eventually, I promise."

*Only for now,* she repeats. *Not for forever?*

"Not for forever," I assure her.

We go back downstairs; Dewey's tail hangs a little lower, her eyes a little less shiny now.

"Let's show Dewey the Puppy Palace!" Macy exclaims.

Dewey looks at me like, *I'd rather not.*

Outside, Dewey stands on the porch, sniffing the air.

"This is your yard," I tell her. "You can run and play . . ."

I lead the way down the steps and walk with Dewey as she explores the perimeter of the yard. When she gets to the back gate she barks once, then looks back at me.

*I remember this—it's the cookie spot!*

Memories of her plate of animal crackers come rushing through my mind. "You're right," I tell her. "How does it feel to be on this side of the fence?"

*Different. But good. Not scary like before.*

I pet her head and ears as we both look out at the woods, and I ask her, "So, do you think you're ready to see the Puppy Palace?"

Her tail falls down flat.

"There might be some more treats in there for you!" I add out loud.

That makes her tail pep back up, and adds a little spring in her step as she follows me to the shed, where Gramps and Macy are already waiting.

She walks in and sniffs at the fleece-lined dog bed, paws at the basket of toys, but doesn't seem very interested. I pull out a stuffed animal squirrel and brand-new bone and show them to her, but she takes each one from my hand and then drops them onto the floor.

She takes one tiny lick of water from her bowl and then sticks her whole face into her empty food bowl. She looks around and turns toward me. *I don't see any cookies?* I giggle.

"What's funny?" Gramps says.

"She's wondering where her treats are."

Gramps reaches for the fresh box of dog biscuits sitting

on the shelf above Mama's worktable and opens the lid. Dewey's nose goes into overdrive sniffing. Gramps hands us each a bone-shaped treat so we can take turns feeding them to her.

"Once you give a dog a treat, you'll be friends forever," he says, stooping over to let Dewey take the biscuit from his hand.

Between the crunching of the biscuits, I can also hear Dewey saying, *Yum, so good!* and *Thank you* as she gently takes the biscuit from Macy. Her tail wags back and forth in time with the sound of her *crunch-crunches*, slobbering as she gobbles every last crumb from the floor.

She sits in her bed and yawns.

"Should we let Dewey get some rest?" Gramps asks.

With that, Dewey's head jerks up and she gives me the saddest puppy eyes. *Does that mean I have to stay here by myself starting now?*

"Gramps, can we let Dewey come back in the house for a little while?"

Gramps scratches his chin, thinking. "I don't know, Sass. We don't want her to get too used to being in the house. We have to set at least some ground rules, don't we?"

I know he's right, but I can't help but pull a sad face on him.

"Tell you what, why don't you both stay out here and

keep Dewey company while I go in and make us some lunch?" Gramps suggests. "How does grilled cheese sound?"

"Good," I answer, and Macy says, "Yum."

But only a minute passes before I hear the screech of the back door, followed by a slam. We hear Gramps calling, "Sadie! Sadie!"

All three of us (me, Macy, and Dewey) jump up and run out of the Puppy Palace.

"Gramps, what's wrong?" I shout to him, as he's rushing toward us.

"Mayday, team," he pants, out of breath. "Elle and Noah just pulled into the driveway!"

"What? Already!" I shout, looking at Dewey, whose tail is pointed straight down, looking back and forth between Gramps and me.

*I'm so sorry, Dewey! I thought we'd have more time. I'll come back later, I promise.*

She whimpers as I close the shed door, but underneath that I hear her say, *Soon?*

That whine. It's the kind of sound that makes my heart sink down into my stomach. She barely even had a chance to be free after getting rescued.

"Soon, Dewey," I answer out loud. "I promise."

I hate that it has to be this way.

## Chapter 22

# STIR-FRIDAY (ON A SATURDAY)

We help bring Gramps's things inside before dinner. When we finish getting everything from the car, Noah flops down on the couch and throws his arm over his face like he's so exhausted.

"I thought there'd be more," I say to no one in particular as we haul stuff from the front door to Gramps's bedroom.

"It would feel like a lot more if *you* had been the one going up and down all those stairs," Noah yells from the couch.

I ignore him and don't even mention the fact that Gramps paid him to help.

"We wanted to bring back more," Mama responds to me, but she keeps looking at Gramps. "But when Katie was called to go in to work, we had a lot less space with only one car. Sorry, Ed. We'll just have to plan another trip, that's all."

"That's fine," Gramps tells her, his tone extra soft. "I appreciate it, Elle."

Mama smiles and then looks to Macy and me as we open up boxes to see what's inside. "For dinner, I was thinking . . . Stir-Friday? Hmm?"

"On a Saturday?" I ask.

"Or I could go order another pizza instead," she teases.

"No!"

"What's a Stir-Friday?" Macy asks.

"It's kind of a little tradition," I explain. "We make different kinds of stir-fry for dinner on Friday nights." Except, now that I think of it, we haven't really done that in a while. I guess Stir-Fridays are another thing—like French toast and mosaics—that has fallen to the wayside lately.

"And so we call them *Stir*-Fridays," I finish.

Mama adds, "We like our puns in this house."

"We're punny," Noah mumbles, sounding like he's half-asleep.

Which makes Macy and Gramps *and* Mama laugh out loud.

"Hey, you stole that from me!" I shout at Noah. Maybe I wouldn't mention his twenty-dollar bribe money, but I wasn't about to let him take credit for my joke.

"Did not!" he shouts back.

"You did too. I made that up so long ago, and you said it was stupid."

He sits up now, and glares at me from the couch. "Whatever."

"Now, Macy," Mama says, talking over us. "Since you're the only child who is not currently giving me a headache, you get to help me decide what to put in the stir-fry. Sound all right?"

Macy nods, and her face can barely contain her smile.

Mama leads her toward the kitchen, and Gramps goes to bring another box to his room, leaving Noah and me alone.

"*Toddler,*" he mutters, and then flops back down on the couch.

"You're the one taking a nap!" Not my best comeback, but he pretends like I didn't say anything anyway.

I think of Dewey, alone outside. All I want to do is go out to the shed to be with her. But as soon as I have that thought, I realize that we're telling each other the same exact thing: *You're not alone.*

**"Stir-Friday on a** Saturday," Mom says as we all sit down at the table together. "I like it—and it's fitting with the way this week has gone, that's for sure."

"What does *that* mean?" Gramps says. I can tell what he's thinking: that him being here this week is what made it so tough. Maybe I would think that too, if I hadn't overheard the pamphlet conversation the other night. If I didn't know that underneath Mom's solid shell she's all soft and worried on the inside.

"Nothing, Dad," Mom responds. "Just that today ended up being kind of like a Friday for me, since I was called in to work."

"Oh," Gramps says, and then brings a forkful of rice and tofu to his mouth.

Mom and Mama share one of their secret-not-so-secret looks.

Mama clears her throat and says, "Well, tonight's Stir-Friday creation was curated by Macy: we have tofu and carrots and zucchini and broccoli, in a secret sauce we made together."

"It's delicious," Mom says. "And healthy—it's perfect."

"Very good," Gramps agrees.

Macy looks down at her plate and turns all rosy in the cheeks.

I hate that there's all this icky weirdness between Mom and Gramps. I wish I could do something to make it better for both of them. Because the thing is, I can see things from *both* of their perspectives: I know what it's like to feel frustrated with your parent the way Mom is frustrated with Gramps, but I also know what it's like to feel like everybody thinks they know what's better for you than you do, and then they go ahead and make decisions for you instead of listening to what *you* want.

Mom sets her fork down and brings her napkin to her mouth before saying, "Sadie, I wanted to tell you, that dog's owners came to pick her up today."

"Oh." I pretend for a second like I don't even remember what she's talking about.

"I thought you'd be happy about it."

Macy gives me a deer-in-headlights look, but Gramps just focuses on his plate of food.

"No. Yeah. I mean good, that's great!" I try to not be either too happy or too unhappy about the news. "I'm glad," I finally say.

**After dinner Macy** and I go to help Gramps organize and sort through his boxes. He shows us a whole box filled with scrapbook after scrapbook of his old newspaper cartoon clippings.

"That's you: E. Mitchell?" Macy says, pointing at Gramps's name beneath the cartoon panels.

"It is," Gramps says, and I can see that it makes him

happy remembering those days, the way he tells us stories about so many of them.

He turns page after page. "Your mother kept every single one and put them in these books so we'd always remember."

"*Mom* did this?" I'm amazed because I can't really picture her sitting down and taking all the time to cut each piece out and arrange it with the date and newspaper headline that accompanied it. She never has that kind of patience: once she tried to help Mama and me with a mosaic, and she got so frustrated she had to leave the She Shed. Mom said she was better at putting animals back together than pieces of glass and ceramic.

"Oh, yes," Gramps says. "Your mother loved to create things, always had a way of making them beautiful."

Now that definitely sounds like Mama, not Mom. So I check to see if that's what he means. "Wait, so Mama put these scrapbooks together for you?"

"What?" he says, looking at me with his forehead all crinkled.

"Do you mean *Mama* made these scrapbooks?" I repeat.

He shakes his head and looks to me and then to Macy, like he's confused. "Who?" he asks.

"You were saying—" I start to explain, but from the doorway, Mom appears.

"Wow, I haven't seen those in a long time," Mom says, taking a step closer to look at the scrapbooks that lay open on Gramps's bed.

"Mom, did you put all of these scrapbooks together of Gramps's art?"

"Me? Gosh, no." She raises her eyebrows. "No, that was all Grandma's handiwork—my mom."

She smiles, but then her eyes drift from me to Macy to Gramps, and then she says, "Girls, Macy's father is going to be picking her up soon, so why don't you go and make sure you have all of your things packed?"


**After Macy leaves,** I go to my desk and open up my laptop. There is an icon in the corner of my screen flashing 13 New Messages.

I click on the icon and open the window.

They are all from Jude.

Now who's not being a great biffle?

> ME: So soooorrryyyy jude! I really meant to get back to you. I'm sorry I hung up on you the other day. I've been so busy with

I immediately start typing what I'm thinking—what I've been wanting to say to her ever since our weird phone call—but then I go back and read all of her messages first.

JUDE: SADIE WHERE ARE
UUUUUUUUUUUUUUUUUUUUUU????

JUDE: I CAN'T EVEN.

JUDE: OKAY.

JUDE: This is HUGE.

JUDE: You know how I told you about Robin and
Lark's cousin, Jordie who's in 6th grade???

No, I don't remember her telling me anything about anyone named Jordie. But I keep reading.

JUDE: well they like me!!! Like, like me LIKE ME. Like
apparently thinks I'm cute WHAT? OMG!!!!!! Robin
told me yesterday and I'm just . . . I don't know

JUDE: This is a butterflyer Sadie! Someone likes me!
idk what to do! Bc I like them too . . . Ahhhhhhhh *I'm
screaming inside*

JUDE: jude + jordie

JUDE: or jordie + jude

JUDE: that's what I've been thinking about ALL day
looooong

JUDE: what should I do??? I'm excited, but super nervous too.

JUDE: I wish you were here! There's SO MUCH to talk about!!!

JUDE: Sadie???

I delete my own message and stare at the blinking cursor, trying to think of what to say. I was so excited to tell her all about Dewey, and I wanted to ask her for an update on Code Name: Winter Break. I was actually feeling so guilty for being mad at her, and now I'm not sure she even realized I was mad to begin with!

I hover my mouse above the X in the corner of the window, looking over Jude's words one last time. I close it without writing anything back.

# Chapter 23

# SIDEKICK

I wake up Sunday morning, and it takes me a minute to remember that I wasn't only dreaming we had succeeded in Code Name: Home, Sweet Home. We actually did it!

I throw the covers off and race to the circle window that looks out over the backyard and woods. Dewey is out there right now. Safe in the She Shed/Puppy Palace. Waiting for me.

"Good morning, Dewey," I whisper, tapping my fingers against the glass.

I step into my frog slippers and bathrobe and hurry down the stairs.

When I reach the kitchen, I see all the ingredients lined up on the counter: eggs, butter, vanilla, powdered sugar, cinnamon. My stomach grumbles just thinking about it. "French toast?" I ask, even before I say good morning.

"Morning, Sade." Mama glances over her shoulder at me from the pantry.

"Not quite," Mom says, holding the loaf of bread in her hand. "I really wanted to make a nice big French toast breakfast this morning, but—" She shows me the bread. There's all this seafoam green that has sprouted along the crust. "Mold."

Normally I would be super disappointed, but right now I have other things that are more pressing. Through the glass door I see Gramps is already outside sitting on the porch, with his heavy flannel jacket and a steaming mug of coffee.

"But," Mama continues, rummaging through the pantry, "we still have all the fixin's for eggs and veggie bacon—"

"Faken!" Noah interrupts from the living room, where he's already playing video games.

"Ah!" Mama exclaims, turning around with a box in her hand. "I found pancake mix!"

Mom takes the box from her, and turns it over, squinting as she points at a spot on the bottom corner. "And it has a perfectly respectable expiration date. Pancakes sound good?"

"Okay," I say, even though pancakes are a poor substitute for French toast, but like I said—there are more important things right now.

While Moms are busy in the kitchen, I slip out the back door to see Gramps. It's chilly this morning, especially without my coat, but the sun is beginning to shine through the trees.

"Psst, Gramps!" I whisper.

"Top of the morning, Sassafras!"

Before I even have to ask, Gramps waves his hand, bidding me to come closer. "Just so you know," he says quietly, "I got up early to feed her before anyone else was awake, and I let her out to do her business—if you know what I mean."

"You're a lifesaver, Gramps!" I accidentally shout. Then, lowering my voice, I ask, "How did she seem? Do you think she slept at all?"

Gramps tilts his head from side to side and says, "So-so, good, but a little nervous. She was happy to see me."

I look toward the shed and sigh. "We have to figure out how we're going to spend time with her today."

He nods. "I have an idea."

**During breakfast, Gramps** says his line, casual, like we planned: "It's such a beautiful fall day outside. Not going to have too many more sunny days like this before it really starts to get cold."

Me: "Yeah, that's true. Actually, Moms, I was telling

Gramps about the trails behind our house, and I know how you don't like me to go walking by myself."

Mom takes a bite of pancake. "Okay?"

"Well, I was thinking since it *is* so nice out, like Gramps said, maybe me and Gramps—or Gramps and I—could go out for a stroll today. Since neither of us would be alone if we're together," I add, throwing in a grin at the end of my sentence.

Mom and Mama share a look. Mama gives a microscopic nod and a half shrug. Mom squints at me, like she's trying to decide something. "Bring your phone, and I want you to look at the time, and be back in one hour. Can you do that?"

I squeal, "Yes."

Mama adds, "Remember, we're trusting you to be very careful, and stick to the paths, and not to go too far."

"I know, we will. I promise!"

I finish my breakfast way too fast, and then race back upstairs to get dressed. I dump all of my school stuff out of my backpack and onto my bedroom floor, so I have room to bring some of Dewey's supplies with us on our walk. I add in my *S. Hawkins* sketchbook and pencils. Gramps says an artist should always keep their tools with them, because you never know when inspiration will strike.

Meanwhile Gramps is doing his part: creating a diversion. He's going to keep Moms and Noah busy while we're getting Dewey out of the shed by asking them to rearrange the furniture in his bedroom.

"Make sure you wear your jackets," Mama calls to us from Gramps's room when she hears the back door open.

"We are!" I shout.

I can hear Dewey already.

*You're here. It was so long. I missed you; I missed you so much!*

I can barely stand how excited I am to see her, and suddenly I'm not sure if what I'm feeling is my excitement or Dewey's. I carefully open the shed door and squeeze inside while Gramps keeps a lookout. Dewey starts whining and jumping up on me, and I have to tell her "shh" while I get her leash clipped onto her collar.

I peek out the window of the shed to see the curtains in Gramps's bedroom are closed—the signal we're all clear. Gramps joins me as I rush to the gate, both of us holding our breath, and we slip out as quickly as possible. It's not until we get to the clearing near the bushes that we stop.

"We made it!" I breathe.

Dewey yelps, and Gramps and I share a big smile because we both understand that was a cry of pure joy. Dewey stands up on her back legs, balancing her front paws on my shoulders so she can kiss my cheek, and as she does, she reminds me, *This is where I found you!*

I see it like a movie playing in my mind, only it's not my

memory—it's Dewey's, and from her point of view, she's the one who found *me*.

"I know," I say out loud. "How could I ever forget?"

"Forget what?" Gramps asks.

"Dewey—she was showing me how this is where we first met."

Along the trail, Dewey crosses back and forth in front of our path, tugging at the leash and sniffing everything, constantly looking back at us and smiling.

"She's never taken a walk like this before. With a person," I add. "On a leash. Just for fun," translating for Gramps everything Dewey is telling me.

*I spent a lot of time walking around the woods, but it was never fun like this.*

She leaps forward, and I have to jog to keep up with her. I yell to Gramps behind us, "She feels like she's seeing it all for the first time with us!"

"Go, run!" he calls. "I'm right behind you."

We run through the dried leaves, our footsteps crunching and making so much noise the birds and squirrels flee as we approach. Dewey slows down as we get close to the pond, and brings us right to the edge of the water.

She's about to get a drink, but I say, "Wait! Dewey, you don't have to drink that water anymore." I slide my backpack off my shoulder and get the plastic collapsible bowl out.

Dewey drinks the whole thing while Gramps and I spread out the blanket.

"This is a good spot," Gramps says, looking out over the water.

"You said we'd come back," I tell him.

He grins at Dewey, then asks me, "She told you you'd come here, did she?"

"No, you did," I say.

"*I* did?" he exclaims, amused. "I think I'd remember that."

"But we were just here a few days ago," I tell him.

Gramps ignores me. He calls Dewey over instead. She comes and lies down between us on the blanket, resting her chin on my knee, as she looks up at me with her different-colored eyes and blinks softly.

*It's okay,* she tells me, sensing my worry.

Gramps reaches into the bag and pulls out a dog biscuit for Dewey, who happily crunches on it while we sit. "What else do you have in there, Sass?" he asks, completely changing the subject.

I pull out my sketchbook and pencils. Dewey sniffs the cover and gives it a lick.

*I don't like that taste.* She smacks her tongue over her mouth.

"It's not food, that's why," I tell her. "It's a story."

"Where are the interstellar adventures of S. Hawkins heading these days?" Gramps asks.

I open my book to the last few pages I was working on and set the book in between us for Gramps to see. "Well," I begin, "S. Hawkins has just landed on planet Earth."

*Keep going.*

"And she can't remember how she got there, or that she was on a mission."

Gramps nods as he turns the page, examining my drawings. "Can't remember, huh?" he asks. "Where'd you come up with that idea?"

"I don't know," I answer, only now realizing I do know: the idea came from Gramps. Dewey is listening, watching me with intense focus.

*What happens next?*

"Well," Gramps smiles slowly. "I certainly recognize this character," he says, pointing at the panel where S. Hawkins sees the dog, and then he reads, *"The first being I meet in this strange new world . . . I shall call it 'Earthling.'"*

He chuckles. "This is great stuff, kiddo. Great stuff."

"Really?"

"Posilutely!" He passes the book back to me and says, "But what happens next?"

"That's what Dewey just asked!"

"Smart dog." Gramps reaches out to pet Dewey's face and she leans into it, closing her eyes.

*Keep telling the story.*

"Well," I say, with my pencil hovering over the blank

page. I start to sketch out the scene as it pops into my mind:

The dog/Earthling leads S. Hawkins into the woods—the fastest way to get to the top of the mountain. Along the way, Earthling shows her the different trees and animals.

"Flora and fauna," Gramps says, watching the story take shape. "Good."

Rabbits—Earthling tells the special agent that one rabbit's name is Dango.

I look up from the drawing. Everything is still and quiet, except the breeze making little ripples on the surface of the pond. I add a lake to the drawing of the forest.

*Fish*, Dewey says, reminding me to add fish to my scene. And just then, there's a tiny splash, bubbles rising to the surface.

Next, a bird swoops down to the ground in front of us and picks up a long pine needle in its beak, flying up to perch in a tree branch right above our heads, where it is building a nest.

"How about that?" Gramps says, clearly seeing the same things I am. He gestures to my sketchbook. "Better get this all down," he tells me.

I scribble my pencil furiously against the paper.

*Look!*

Dewey's head pops up from Gramps's lap, at attention.

There, on the trunk of a tree with a big leafy nest, two squirrels climb and chase each other.

"How is this happening?" I say out loud. "Where are they all coming from?"

"Don't ask me," Gramps replies. "Ask your sidekick there."

A toad leaps from the bank of the pond to a log that's half-submerged under water. I quickly sketch each of them, as fast as my hand will let me. I don't want to miss any detail.

"Dewey, are you doing this?" I ask as I watch, mesmerized.

*Wait for it . . . here it comes again!*

She looks at the water and barks at the exact moment another fish bursts out of the surface and splashes back under again. Animals surround us—they chatter and twitch and sniff, inspecting us. A tiny chipmunk scrambles onto the blanket and sniffs Dewey's tail.

"This is like magic," I whisper.

Dewey seems to smile as she raises her head to look at me. I draw a thought bubble over the scene and record her words: *It's not magic. This is how things always are.*

Just then, my phone rings in my pocket, and all the animals scatter away from us like leaves in the wind.

It rings again.

"H-hello?" I answer.

It's Mom. "Sadie, you should've been home almost twenty minutes ago." I pull my phone away from my face to look at the time—I don't know how it went by so fast. "Everything okay?"

"Yeah," I answer. "Everything's fine; we'll head home soon."

I hang up and look around.

"Gramps, you saw all of that too, right?" I ask, because I'm honestly not sure if my imagination was running wild or not.

"I did," he says, nodding. "It's pretty amazing what can happen when you take the time to sit still and just pay attention to what's around you."

"Yeah," I agree, rubbing the soft part behind Dewey's ears. It's as soft as the real Dango's fur.

"Like I always say, inspiration's everywhere when you look for it." Gramps begins to maneuver to his knees, and Dewey leaps up to position herself beside him as he finds his balance. "Now, let's get me home before I turn into a pumpkin."

## Chapter 24

# THIS IS NOT A FIRE DRILL

Lying in bed, I think about what Gramps said earlier in the woods about my graphic novel: *Great stuff.* Maybe I let Bailey's stunt on the bus at the beginning of the year make me feel like my story, my drawings, were dumb and babyish. But today, when I was drawing with Dewey and Gramps there, inspiration just flowing in from all around us—it didn't feel dumb. It felt . . . important.

I drift off into a dream of S. Hawkins, and her journey across the mountain with her loving sidekick, who she keeps calling Earthling.

*That's not my name, you know*, is the last thing I remember thinking before I fall completely asleep.

At some point, it morphs into a school dream—those are the worst! But suddenly there's an alarm going off in class. Ms. Avery shouts at everyone to stay in their seats. "It's just a fire drill," she yells. Only I'm not S. Hawkins anymore. I'm just me. And Macy is standing next to me saying, "You need to wake up! Now!"

My eyes flutter open. I'm not at school; I'm in my room. There is an alarm blaring, but instead of Macy, it is Noah standing over me, shaking my shoulders.

"Get up!"

"Just a fire drill," I mumble.

"This is not a fire drill!" he yells, pulling on my arm. "We have to get downstairs now!"

As my feet hit the floor, I'm fully awake, and the alarm is real. Loud. It's so piercing I have to cover my ears.

"Come on, come on!" Noah shouts over the noise, grabbing on to my hand and holding it tightly.

In the hallway, Moms stumble out of their room and yell, "Are you okay? You got your sister?" Mom leads the way down the stairs, and Mama follows close behind us.

The kitchen is filled with smoke. Mom throws open the back door and ushers us outside, yelling, "Be careful, but hurry!"

It's all happening so fast I don't even realize that she's gone back inside at first, until Mama yells, "You two stay here!" She pulls the neckline of her shirt up over her mouth and nose and follows Mom.

Noah is still holding on to my hand—I squeeze it. "Noah?" I cry.

"It's okay," he says. "They're just getting Gramps."

After what feels like way too long for my moms to be inside of a smoke-filled house, Mom and Mama emerge with Gramps, each of them holding one of his arms to help him down the porch steps.

"Gramps, are you okay?" I shout, running toward him.

He looks around like he's not sure how he got outside. Mom has gone back in again and is opening windows, letting the smoke come billowing out.

"Mama!" I shriek. "Make Mom come back outside with us!"

"It's all right." She pulls me into a hug. "Somebody left the stove on. But there's no fire, just a lot of smoke. Mom's getting the air to circulate so the alarm will stop."

"Who left the stove on?"

But as soon as the question is out of my mouth, I know the answer. I look up at Mama, and Noah, who is now standing next to us, and they are both staring at Gramps.

The alarm stops. But the silence it leaves behind feels even louder.

We stand there, not speaking, barely breathing.

I don't know how much time passes before Mom appears in the doorway, swinging a towel through the air to fan the smoke. She calls to us, "I think it's okay to come in."

We file into the still slightly smoky kitchen, and I see the kettle sitting on the counter all charred and battered. Mama sits at the table. Gramps too. Noah leans against the fridge. And I take a seat next to Gramps.

"Dad," Mom says, pacing as she waves her hand at the stove. "What happened?"

"I—" he begins, but immediately stops. "I don't know. Why do you assume it was me?"

"Because, Ed," Mama says, "you were the only one down here."

"I—I think," he stutters through the words, "I was making your tea, Katie."

"Dad, I didn't ask you to make me tea."

"Yes, you did," he argues. "You couldn't sleep. And I must have . . . forgotten about it. I dozed off."

"I didn't *ask* you to make me tea," she repeats more firmly.

"What do you want from me?" he says in a gruff voice, suddenly standing from his chair. "What are you accusing me of?"

"Dad," Mom begins, but Gramps cuts her off.

"No! You—you're keeping me here against my will. You expect me to be able to get settled in here without any of my belongings? I'm living out of a suitcase, for crying out loud! Of course I'm out of sorts—anyone would be!" he yells.

Mama looks startled, and she stands up now too. "Lower your voice, Ed," she says to him. "The kids."

"Dad, what are you talking about?" Mom shouts. "You do have your things here."

"Remember, we went to get them already," Mama tells him. "We're going to go back to get the rest, but—"

"Really?" he snaps, crossing his arms. "When?"

"I—I don't know," Mama answers.

"I'll tell you when: never!" He thumps his fist against the counter, making us all jump. "It will never happen, because you don't want me here to begin with."

Mom has sat down at the table and rests her head in her hands.

"Mom?" I whisper, setting my hand on her shoulder. She pats it once, but doesn't say anything.

Mama continues, "I know things are probably confusing for you right now—"

"Confusing?" Gramps yells, cutting Mama off. "I'm not confused at all! I think you're the one who's confused!"

"You know we're all on the same side here, Ed," Mama says in her firm yet understanding teacher voice.

Mom straightens up in her chair, but when she speaks her voice is frayed and small. "You know, Dad, this is an adjustment for everyone, but we can't start lashing out at each other."

Mama lets out a sigh and says, "Kids, everything is okay,

all right? Noah, why don't you take Sadie back upstairs?"

Noah nods and murmurs, "Okay," and motions for me to come with him. I turn back to look at Gramps, and I don't even recognize him right now. I follow Noah up the stairs, but I can still hear them as Noah walks me to my bedroom.

"Why don't you just ship me off to an old folks' home and be done with it?" Gramps's voice is muffled, but I can still pick up this sharp bite to his words. "Isn't that where this is all leading anyway?"

"Don't say that," Mama scolds.

"That's not what anyone wants," Mom says. "What we want is to make this work, but you've got to—"

"Forget it," Gramps interrupts. "I'm going to my room, if that's okay with you. I'm sorry, the *guest room*."

"Ed . . ." Mama calls after him, just as Mom is saying, "Dad, come back!"

But there's no response.

I climb into bed, and Noah even comes in and picks my blankets up off the floor from when they fell in the commotion.

"Noah?"

"Yeah."

"I'm scared."

He looks at me, and in this moment there's no trace of

his mean older-brother-bully self. He's just him again, and I know he understands because I can see in his eyes that he's scared too, even if he tries to act brave and tough.

"Want me to stay in here with you?" he asks, but he doesn't wait for me to answer before he's sitting down on the partially deflated air mattress that I never put away after Macy slept over.

"Thanks, Noah," I whisper, as I lie down.

I hear Dewey bark outside. I try to fall back asleep, but even though it's silent, I can still hear the sound of Gramps yelling, the sounds of that alarm echoing in my ears.

## Chapter 25

# THE MONDAYS (TIMES A MILLION)

When I come downstairs the next morning, Gramps is sitting in the living room with a mug of coffee, and the newspaper spread open in front of his face. Normally, I'd go sit next to him. But today doesn't feel normal.

I take a seat at the table and pour myself some cereal, watching Gramps out of the corner of my eye. Noah sits down next to me, gives me a half smile and a "Hey."

No jokes or mean remarks. Just "hey."

I respond with my own half smile.

*"It's like last night never even happened,"* Mom whispers to Mama as she walks behind her to reach into the fridge for her half-and-half.

"Yep," Mama murmurs back.

I want to act like it never happened either.

**I meet Macy** at the corner of my street where she's waiting for me. It's hard to stand still at the bus stop because it's chilly again, so we keep moving to stay warm. Macy sways back and forth, and I bounce up and down, my teeth chattering.

Now that I'm out of my house, there's this overwhelming wave of sadness that washes over me.

Macy frowns. "What's wrong?"

"Gramps had a hard night." I shake my head, trying to blink away little pinpricks of tears. "I don't really want to talk about it."

Macy nods—of course she understands not wanting to talk about something that's upsetting. And now I do too.

"I've been trying to talk to Dango," she says out of nowhere, changing the subject.

I'm so thankful to have something else to think about. "Is it working?" I ask.

"It's hard to tell. I'm not sure if I'm just making things up in my head or if he's really talking to me."

"That's how I felt at first, too."

"How did you know for sure, then?" she asks me, wrapping her scarf around her neck one more time.

"I guess because Dewey started to tell me things I couldn't have already known, like her name and how she was in trouble and needed help," I answer. "Has Dango said anything that you couldn't have known about?"

She looks off into the distance like she's thinking and says, "No. Maybe it's just a thing between you and Dewey."

The bus comes rumbling down the street toward us. I sigh, thinking of all the hours that I'll have to go through before we're dropped back off again.

"Stupid block of cheese on wheels," Macy says, which makes me laugh, even through my chattering teeth.


**I spend most** of the day staring out of the windows in our classroom. Dewey pops into my thoughts and I imagine what she's doing—Gramps feeding her breakfast, or running around the backyard—and then my imagination sort of takes over the way it does sometimes. A little scene plays in my mind of Gramps hanging out with Dewey in the Puppy Palace, Dewey curled up in her warm bed while Gramps sits at Mama's desk with a big sketchpad, drawing. Then I imagine I'm there too, sitting on the floor next to Dewey. She looks up at me, with her tongue sticking out of the side of her mouth.

"Sadie? Sadie!"

Something snaps me back to the classroom.

"*Sadie*," a voice says again.

"Huh?" I say. "What?"

Ms. Avery is standing in front of me, with this weird

bulging vein in her neck, looking super frustrated. "I said, where is your homework?"

I glance around. We're on math, apparently. I look down at my desk—I have my social studies book open.

"Sorry, I—" I stutter, rooting around in my desk cubby, trying to find my math book. "I have it; I'll get it out."

She looks like she wants to say more, or maybe even send me to the principal's office again. But instead, she walks back up to the front of the room. I'm in so much trouble if Moms hear about this.

I look over at Macy—her whole face is contorted. "I tried to get your attention," she whispers.


**I can't shake** this fog that seems to be surrounding me today—or maybe it's more like smoke, invisible but lingering on me from last night. When we get off the bus, Macy and I walk together until we get to her street, and then we have to go our separate ways because she said her Grandma told her she's going to wear out her welcome.

I race home, trying to outrun the fog.

"I'm home!" I yell as I cross the backyard.

Dewey comes running out to greet me.

*You were gone so long!*

"I know," I tell her as I crouch down to give her a big hug.

*I thought you might never come back.*

She sniffs me all over, her tail wagging so hard against my legs that it hurts.

*I missed you so much today.*

Gramps joins us. "I kept her company until you got home. Or rather, she kept me company."

*He was fine today*, Dewey tells me, answering the question on my mind.

"Thank you," I whisper to her as I bury my face in her coat.

Gramps stoops to pat Dewey's head, and then mine. I don't know what to say, but thankfully Gramps does the talking. "You really did find yourself a good dog, Sassafras."

I look up at him; he seems happy, normal, not a trace of the person I saw in the kitchen last night.

"Now, you two enjoy each other," he says. "I'm going to go inside and warm up my bones. I'll give you a heads-up when it's time, okay?"

That smoky fog lifts away, and things begin to feel normal again. I start to think that maybe last night wasn't all that terrible. It was an accident. Everybody has accidents sometimes. Besides, that fire alarm got to all of us, dialing our nerves up to the maximum. Everyone was upset.

I watch as he heads toward the house, and I call after him, "Thanks, Gramps!"

"Welcome, kiddo!" he yells back with a wave.

*We're okay*, I think to myself. *We're going to be okay. I'm more than okay!*

Dewey bounces up and down in front of me with her ball in her mouth before she drops it at my feet. I throw it and she chases, but she doesn't quite understand about bringing it back to me. She's more interested in running through the piles of leaves. I can feel how much fun she's having, so I join in. We jump, and the leaves fly all around us. Then I gather them up again. We do this over and over, until we're too tired to get back up.

We lie there next to each other, looking up at the sky, which is blue and full of white puffy clouds that remind me of Macy's bedroom ceiling. I wish time could pass as slowly now as it does when I'm in school.

"Dewey, I was wondering, how did you get your name? Where did you live before you found me? Did you have a family?"

Her story comes into my mind like a memory. I can see her outside of a house, with a chain-link fence all around the yard. She has a wooden doghouse that smells like mold and sits under a big tree in the shade so the ground never fully dries.

She's always cold and wet.

I can see the people she's talking about, and they're not very nice. They never let her inside, and they don't feed her enough or give her clean water.

*They wanted me to be a guard dog. But I wasn't very good at it.*

The mean people want her to be scary so no one tries to come to their door, but she's too friendly and lets someone in the gate. The people yell at her, and tie her to the doghouse with a rope so she can't walk around very far in any direction.

They never pet her or even talk to her, but they talk about whether or not they should keep her. They look at her and say, "Do we?" And she barks. That is the only time they look at her and speak.

*So that's how I got my name.*

She shows me what had happened on her last night there: It was raining and lightning and thundering so loud she pulled on the rope so hard that it broke. She scratched on the door to be let inside because she was scared.

The mean people yelled at her again, and instead of letting her in, they pushed her outside of the gate in the pouring rain and told her, "Get! Go!"

She was so scared and so lonely. She cried, but nobody paid attention.

She walked around for a long time, hiding, finding things to eat out of garbage cans. Sometimes she would meet people, but they were never nice. She could always hear what they were thinking, but they could never hear her.

I shiver with the memories, and pull Dewey closer to me in the pile of leaves.

*Don't be sad.* She licks my face. *Because then I found you and you could hear me. And now we're together and I'm not cold and scared anymore.*

"Dewey," I say out loud, petting her spotted fur. "I love you so much."

I hug Dewey tight, trying to gather up her whole body in my arms, and focus on sending her all the love in my heart, so she knows what it feels like to be loved—that it's more than a word.

The back door screeches open. Both Dewey and I look over at Gramps. "Sadie, it's time!"

Even Dewey knows what that means.

We jump up from the pile of leaves, and the air feels so cold now that we're not close. I don't want to do it, but I bring Dewey back to the shed and she goes inside and sits down on her bed and looks at me with the most patient and understanding eyes.

"I'll be back," I tell her. "I promise."

**I try to** do some homework, but I don't get very far before I hear the *bloopbloop* sound coming from my laptop.

Jude.

I haven't found a chance to write her back. Or maybe there have been chances; I just haven't wanted to take any of them. There's another *bloopbloop*, followed by a ding, which means she left me a message.

I don't check it.

I flip through *S. Hawkins*, making a few notes here and there, but I'm still too distracted by everything to work on much. I think about Dewey, and the people who treated her so badly. I think of Gramps and last night and how mad he was. I think about how I'm going to have to find more ways to spend time with Dewey, and how that means more lies to Moms. Inside, all the goodness of playing with Dewey in the leaves is filled with something empty and sad.

Instead, I go to bed early, just wanting this weirdly sad day to be over. The house is quiet; everyone is in bed. I close my eyes and try to sleep, but all I can see are Dewey's memories of the mean people who never even bothered to give her a proper name.

## Chapter 26

# THE DOG
# FORMERLY KNOWN
# AS DEWEY

Tuesday is a brand-new day. It's still cold, but the sun is shining through my bedroom window and the smell of smoke has finally made its way out of the house. I even decide to bring *S. Hawkins* with me to school again—no more being embarrassed of it!

During lunch I fill Macy in on all of the sad things Dewey showed me yesterday. But I tell Macy not to be too upset about it, because there's something starting to take shape in my thoughts. The outline of it is there in my mind.

"I can't quite tell what," I say. "But it's something *good.*"

"Hmm," Macy murmurs. "Sort of like when you can almost remember a dream, but then it floats away."

"Exactly like that," I tell her.

I pull my sketchbook out and flip through the pages.

"Hey, I remember seeing that once," Macy says.

"Yeah, when Bailey passed it around on the bus."

"Oh, yeah." Macy cringes. "Well, forget about that. This is really cool—I wish I could draw like you," she tells me, admiring the pages. "Is S. Hawkins supposed to be you?" she asks.

"I didn't think so when I first came up with her," I explain. "I took her name from the title of one of Mama's mosaics. Last year she had one of her mosaics in an art gallery with a whole bunch of other artists' work. She titled it *Sadie Hawkins Dance* as a secret message between the two of us, because I helped make it and because it includes my name."

"What is a Sadie Hawkins Dance?" Macy asks.

"It's a real thing that old people remember where the girls would ask people to dances, which I guess was unusual back then. I don't think there is such a thing now because it doesn't really matter who asks who to a dance anymore."

Macy nods.

"So that's where the name came from anyway, but I guess along the way she has become more like me— I mean, a much cooler version of me." I giggle. "But still."

"You're pretty cool, even if you can't time travel," Macy tells me.

On the next page, there's a note I scribbled last night before bed: *Earthling has just told S. Hawkins that "Earthling" is not its name.*

"Macy, I've got it!" I say, grabbing onto her hand.

"What?" she gasps.

"Dewey's name," I say. "Think about it: names should be special and thoughtful, not just some random words someone says at you!" I shout, getting excited. "Look at us: our middle names are both after real people."

"Right," Macy says, quietly at first, then louder, "you're so right! And it goes the other way too. Names that *aren't* nice"—she shoots eye daggers at the side of Bailey's head—"are so awful."

"Dewey needs a new name."

**Getting off the** bus, our feet barely touch the ground as we race to my house. Gramps is sitting on the back porch, Dewey lying at his feet in a ray of sunlight. She jumps at the sound of the door opening, and I immediately get on my hands and knees to give her a good bear hug.

*You're home.*

"There she is!" Gramps says. "I told you she'd be coming home soon."

*I missed you!*

Dewey's so excited she leaps off of the porch and runs

into the yard through piles of leaves to get her ball.

"I missed you too, Dewey!" I yell, and Macy and I run after her.

Gramps calls from the top step of the porch, "You girls stay out here with her, and I'll fix us up a little after-school snack—we'll have it alfresco?"

"Who's Al Fresco?" I yell back.

Gramps bursts out laughing and swishes his hand at me, saying, "You get me every time!" as he walks back toward the house.

Dewey brings the ball to Macy this time, and she throws it. "You two like to joke around a lot," she says to me. "It's nice."

Dewey runs back and sits between us. We take turns petting her.

"Don't you have fun with your grandma?" Dewey looks at Macy too, waiting for her response.

"Sometimes." She shrugs. "But it seems different with your gramps. Like, you two have fun together. Like you're friends. My sobo is more of a . . . *traditional* grandma."

"What's that like? I don't have any grandmothers."

"Well, like she's always cooking the most amazing foods and leaving little surprise gifts around the house for me, and she teaches me a lot, and helps with homework and school—that's very important to her." She emphasizes that last part with her tongue stuck out to the side and wide eyes that she suddenly crosses in toward her nose, like she's done way too many math problems.

"But," she continues, "she definitely wouldn't have helped me rescue a dog, that's for sure!"

Dewey lifts her head and gives us a big doggy grin. *I'm glad I found you first!*

"Dewey," I say. "We're going to pick out a new name for you!"

She blinks twice.

"What's she saying?" Macy whispers.

"Nothing."

I continue. "A new name for a new life," I tell Dewey. "A fresh start. What do you think?"

*I don't know; will it hurt?*

"No, silly, it doesn't hurt."

Macy mutters, "Aww."

"We just think there's a better name for you, one that fits your personality." I'm not sure if she knows what *personality* really means, because she turns her head. "You should have a name that, when you hear it, you know you're loved."

She nuzzles her head under my chin and lets out the tiniest happy whimper. *I think I would like that very much.*

"Does that mean she likes the idea?" Macy asks.

Dewey barks, using her full voice, and licks Macy's hand. I don't need to translate what that means.

Gramps comes out with a plate of PB&J triangles and Dewey's favorite: animal crackers. Dewey races toward him and he throws her an animal cracker, which she catches midair. The four of us sit around the patio table, taking bites of PB&J, trying to think of some good names.

"Bella?" Gramps suggests.

"Lucy?" Macy says. "No. How about Daisy?"

"No," I say. "She's not quite a Daisy."

"Freckles," Gramps says, "because of her spots?"

Macy shakes her head and makes a face.

"Blue—because of her one blue eye?" Macy tries.

"Priscilla?"

"She just doesn't act like a Priscilla, though."

"Parker? Marley?"

I shake my head.

"Luna!" Gramps offers.

I look at Dewey. *Luna?*

She sneezes.

"I don't think she likes that one."

"Nora?" he tries again. "Or Dora?"

She sneezes twice.

"Lizzie!" Macy shouts. "Cocoa?"

Before I can veto of any those suggestions, the doorbell rings from inside the house. We all freeze. I look at Gramps. "Sit tight, I'll go check." Gramps stands from his chair and goes to open the back door, sticking his head out to say, "I'll give a signal if you need to hide—the Dog Formerly Known as Dewey."

We try to see through the window, but it's hard to get a clear view of the door from this angle outside. Dewey paces back and forth.

I can hear Gramps talking, and then there's another voice that I kind of recognize.

"I can't tell who it is," I whisper.

Macy gasps. "I can!"

Gramps opens the door, and Macy's grandmother steps out onto the deck with a big smile. "Surprise." She's carrying a plate of something covered in what looks like many layers of plastic wrap.

"Sobo, what are you doing here?" Macy asks.

"I decided I would walk over to pick you up." Then she leans into Gramps and whispers, "I wanted to make sure my Mieko—*Macy*—is not wearing out her welcome."

"Never," Gramps says.

"Oh, good," she coos. "I brought treats, just in case. Here," she says, pulling off the plastic. She passes the plate to Gramps, and his eyes brighten.

"Sobo," Macy says gently, but I can tell by her bright

pink cheeks that she's mortified. "You didn't have to—"

"I want to," she interrupts, but then catches sight of Dewey. "And who is this?"

Gramps intervenes. "This is our new dog. We're still thinking of names, but she came with the name Dewey."

Macy's grandma purses her lips as she looks at Dewey, and then shakes her head, saying, "No, you are right. That is not her name."

Macy's sobo is cooler than Macy thinks.

"It's mochi. Try," she says, waving her hand at the food.

"Don't mind if I do," Gramps says first, selecting one of the sweets. "Please, sit down. The girls were just playing with, uh . . ."

"Not Dewey," she finishes.

"Yum," Gramps mumbles into his bite, then asks her, "What did you call these again, moch-as?"

"Mochi," I correct.

"Mochi," Gramps repeats, then looks at Dewey. *"Mochi?"*

Dewey turns her head and barks.

"We'll keep thinking on names," Gramps says.

"Go play," Macy's grandma tells her. "But homework later, yes?"

"Yes," Macy agrees.

We take that as our cue to go out into the yard, leaving Gramps and Sobo to talk.

Not-Dewey's big foxtail waves back and forth, and she seems so happy, I never would have guessed she'd ever been unhappy. In this moment, surrounded by laughter and the scent of leaves and the crisp coldness in our breath, sugary sweetness on my tongue, I can't believe *I* had been so unhappy not too long ago either.

## Chapter 27

# SOME RULES ARE
# MEANT TO BE BROKEN

During school on Wednesday, it starts to rain. The sheets of water crash down against the windows so loud it's hard for everyone to concentrate today, not just me.

I worry about Dewey being all alone, especially after everything she showed me.

After school, I accidentally leave my umbrella on the bus, so Macy shares hers with me. We run as fast as we can, tromping through puddles, and end up completely soaked by the time we make it to my house, even with the umbrella. We take our shoes off at the door because they are filled with pools of rainwater.

Gramps is standing at the living room windows looking out at the Puppy Palace. When he sees how soaked we are, he says, "Gee, did you gals swim here or what?"

"Practically!" I say. "How's Dewey doing with this rain?"

Gramps gets us towels to set all of our wet things on. "I checked on her about an hour ago, and she was all right. A little nervous. But not terrible."

I clasp my hands together, my hair dripping onto my shoulders. "Gramps, just this once, do you think we could bring her inside—please?" I plead.

Gramps looks back and forth between Macy and me. Finally he answers, "I suppose some rules are meant to be broken. But we have to make sure she's out of here well before your moms get home."

Gramps starts getting into his raincoat and rubber boots, while Macy and I race upstairs and throw on whatever mismatched clothes I see first in my closet. I'm in pajama pants and an ugly knitted holiday sweater, and Macy's in sweatpants and my favorite Supergirl hoodie.

We're downstairs in time to see Dewey standing at the back door looking like a wet mop with a face, while Gramps is still making his way through the yard. I grab one of the towels and wrap Dewey up inside of it.

"There you go," I tell her. "I'll get you warm and dry."

Macy grabs another towel and we pat her down together, but then Dewey shakes her body and sprays rainwater *everywhere*.

Macy exclaims, "Yuck!"

*I couldn't help it!* And then she shakes again, involuntarily skidding across the kitchen floor. "It's okay," I tell her, and then I shake my wet hair too. Macy lets out another laugh-shriek.

Gramps comes in through the door, and somehow, he's stayed mostly dry. "Oh, good, I can see you're not getting overly excited about the dog coming inside."

Dewey is cautious as she ventures into the house. I spot Catniss before she does. She stalks along the back of the couch, watching Dewey's every move. When Dewey catches sight of her, she whines and hides behind me.

*You have a cat?*

"Oh, don't worry about Catniss, Dewey," Gramps hangs his coat over a kitchen chair and sits on the couch. He holds his hand out, and Catniss rubs her face against his hand. "She's a big softie once you get to know her."

Macy joins Gramps, and I coax Dewey to follow.

*I thought you liked other animals?* I ask her, remembering the day at the pond.

Dewey looks up at me through her long doggy eyelashes, and I can feel how nervous she is about Catniss. *It's not because she's a cat—it's because she's a family member.*

"You're a family member too," I say out loud. But I know that's not exactly true yet.

I sit cross-legged on the floor, and Dewey sits in my lap like she's some kind of a mini teacup dog. I wrap my arms around her and try my best to tell her with my thoughts that Catniss is a friend. "Right, Catniss?" I say out loud.

Catniss slinks off the couch and walks toward Dewey with a little meow, but Dewey won't look at her; she buries her face under my arm. I kiss her soft forehead and then try to raise her chin, but she keeps her eyes closed.

I don't know if Catniss can hear me the way Dewey does, but I plead with her, *Please, Catniss. Be nice.*

Catniss sits down in front of us and yawns with a big tigerlike stretch, then sets her paw on Dewey's tail. It swishes back and forth once. Dewey glances at Catniss but turns back to me right away. Catniss climbs up onto my leg and paws at Dewey like she's tapping on her shoulder.

"Look," I whisper. "She wants to be friends."

Dewey blinks her blue and brown eyes at me, then slowly turns toward Catniss. Catniss touches her nose to Dewey's, reaches out with her paw, and boops her on the head. Dewey flinches but leans in for a sniff. Catniss boops her again and gently grabs Dewey's face between her paws and licks her cheek. Dewey's stiff expression loosens into a big doggy smile with her signature look: tongue hanging out of the side of her mouth. Catniss jumps down and immediately starts rolling around on the floor, belly up.

Dewey slowly squirms off my lap and lies down next to her.

"They like each other!" Macy squeals, clasping her hands together.

"See?" I say out loud. "Friends."

*Sisters*, Dewey tells me. *She says we're sisters!*

"Sisters!" I agree. "She's right."

Once the newness of Catniss wears off, Dewey can't keep her eyes open, and soon both Dewey and Catniss are curled up around each other, asleep on the carpet.

"They have the right idea," Gramps says. "You girls will be all right if I go lie down for a little catnap of my own?" he asks.

"Sure, Gramps," I answer. As he stands up, he has to steady himself with one hand on the coffee table and the other on the arm of the couch. I remember how Mama had said that some things might change with Gramps, like he might get tired more easily than he used to.

I stand up and hold my hand out.

Gramps looks at my hand like it smells bad. "What are you doing?" he asks.

"It's just that, I thought, maybe"—*you need help*, but I don't say that—"I mean, do you not feel well?"

"Sass, you're starting to sound like your mother. I feel fine, just tired." He shoos his hand in my direction.

I watch as Gramps makes his way down the hall to

his room. I definitely don't want to start sounding like my mother, especially when she and Gramps haven't been getting along too great lately.

Dewey sighs and opens her eyes. *Where'd he go?*

"It's okay, he's just taking a nap," I say.

"My grandma takes naps too," Macy responds, even though I wasn't exactly talking to her. "She says naps are good for you."

Macy and I are careful to be quiet, with all the napping going on. We decide to make some decorations for Gramps's room, now that it looks like he's staying for good. She shows me how to make the same kind of paper garland she has hanging in her bedroom. We get a big stack of old newspapers from the recycling bin and sit on the floor and fold what seem like hundreds of origami flowers and cranes and stars.

"How did you learn to do this?" I ask her. Part of me wonders if it was something her mom had shown her, and maybe that's why she likes doing it so much, but I haven't quite figured out how to bring up her mom again. "Did someone teach you?" I ask instead.

"No, I just learned from videos online," she says. "And books too."

"Oh, that's cool. I thought maybe it was like a family tradition sort of thing."

"Not really. After my mom, you know, passed," she

begins, "I wanted to learn more about my Japanese side and found all these videos about it. My counselor said it might be good to learn how to do something crafty— like it would help with my anxiety. I just keep doing it. And I guess, in a way, it sort of makes me feel closer to my mom."

"That makes sense." I think about it for a minute, and tell her, "I had a lot of school anxiety at the beginning of the year. Drawing helps me with that stuff too."

"Yeah," Macy agrees. She opens her mouth like she was going to say something more, but then closes it and looks away.

"What?" I ask her.

"It's kind of weird," she cautions, her eyes meeting mine once again. "But I actually have a special plan at school. For my anxiety stuff."

"What kind of plan?" I ask.

"Like, I'm allowed to be late sometimes, or leave the classroom for a few minutes if I need to get up and walk around. And that's why Ms. Avery never says anything about my origami-ing during class and—wait, why are you looking at me like that?" she says, stopping in the middle of her sentence. "Your eyes are all big, and you're staring at me like you stuck your finger in an electrical socket!"

"Sorry," I start. "It's just—do you have something called an IEP?"

"Ye-yeah," she stutters. "You know about those?"

"I have one too. But mine is because I have this learning di—" I start to say disability, but then I switch it at the last second to the word Moms say—"*difference*. Which is also part of why I was having such bad anxiety about school." I swallow and clear my throat. "You know, my lessons?"

Macy nods.

"I actually have to go to the Resource Room on those days, for *math* lessons. Sorry if I let you think I was going for music lessons."

"It's okay. I mean, I sort of let you think I had doctor's appointments, didn't I?" she tells me. "But it was only because I thought I was the only one in our class with an IEP."

"Me too." I feel my face beaming at her. "Is it weird that it makes me feel so much better knowing you have one too?"

"No." She shakes her head and chuckles. "It makes me feel better too."

One more unexpected thing that we have in common.

We're quiet as we focus on the garland again. But I realize that this is the first time all school year I don't feel bad about my IEP. Outside there's a distant rumble of thunder that wakes Catniss. She starts grooming Dewey, licking the top of her head, and then they fall deeper into sleep.

The rain doesn't let up at all. It just gets darker and gloomier.

A car door slams. Catniss purrs and leaps over the back of the couch, prancing toward the front door.

"Mom!" I shout.

We jump into action. Dewey wakes up but is confused. I try to explain in my thoughts what's going on. She follows us to the door but hesitates to step out into the rain.

"Hurry!" I say.

Macy and I both go out with her, neither of us having time to put on our raincoats or even our shoes. We run out to the shed and get Dewey inside.

"I'm sorry!" I shout over the rain. "I'm so sorry, I know you're scared, but I'll be right inside the whole time."

*But—*

"I'm sorry," I repeat. "I have to."

I look to Macy, and I know she can read my thoughts in this moment too, because all I can think is, *I can't do it.*

Macy steps between us and closes it for me, saying, "Here, let me."

We are racing back to the house, when Mom appears at the door. "What on earth are you doing?" she asks. By the time we get back inside, Mom is standing there with her hands on her hips, waiting for an explanation.

"Hi, Mom," I say, pretending I don't see anything strange about what's happening, pretending that the drops of water on my cheeks are from the rain and not from the tears I'm fighting back. I swallow hard.

"Do you want to tell me why you two are running around outside in the freezing rain without coats?" She looks down at the puddles that are forming around us. "Or shoes?"

"Well, our shoes were still all wet from walking home from school earlier, and we just felt like playing in the rain," I lie. "It was fun, right?"

"Right," Macy mutters.

"Go get dried off, and change into some warm clothes— I'm not sending Macy home drenched from head to toe," she snaps, looking more and more annoyed by all the newspaper everywhere and our piles of wet coats and school bags still laying by the door.

"And where is your grandfather, anyway?" She picks up the sleeve of his wet raincoat and shakes her head.

"Oh, he's—"

"I'm right here," Gramps says.

"We were making some decorations for Gramps's room," I tell Mom. "See?"

"And running around in the rain," she adds. "Go on

and get dried off. Put everything in the laundry room, and we'll get Macy's clothes back to her after we wash them."

Mom doesn't notice that Macy is already wearing my clothes, but that's probably a good thing: fewer questions.

Ugh. I place my hand over my stomach. It feels like the lies bounce around inside me, making me suddenly queasy.

Macy places her hand on my shoulder. "Dewey will be okay."

I nod, but I'm not so sure.

# Part Four

# SERENDIPITY

## Chapter 28

# THE STORM

It's still raining when I wake up in the morning. All night long, I had nightmares about Dewey in her old life, chained up outside, drenched in her mildewy doghouse. I shake the dream from my mind as I get out of bed and go to the circle window. Dewey is safe.

I purposely take my time getting ready so Mama has to drive me to school with her and Noah. I don't think I can ride the bus today without Macy. It seems like forever until she arrives at school, because of her Thursday morning appointment.

But when she finally does, she gives me a small wave and immediately pulls out a piece of paper and starts writing. She looks up at Ms. Avery, but all the while she's actually folding it up into a triangle without even looking.

When Ms. Avery turns around, she passes me the note.

*Sadie,*

*Bad news. I can't come over after school today. I have to help my grandma with some stuff at home that I promised I would do.*
    *Sorry* ☹

                                    *—m.m.m.*

When I read her note, I feel exactly like the weather outside.

*NOOOOOOO! WHYYYYYY? We'll miss you— remember we still need to figure out a name for (the dog formerly known as) Dewey. R U sure you can't help her later?*

Macy writes back:

*Well, the truth is she needs me to dye her hair for her. She says I do it better because she can't see the back of her head. But really, it's our special "girl time" together. It's kinda fun, but I will miss hanging out with the team, though!*

I can't be upset about that. I draw a little picture of Macy's grandma with fancy hair, and pass the note back to Macy.

The day drags on and on.

In the cafeteria at lunch, the power goes out with a big zap and everything goes dark. There's tons of screaming, a lunch tray clatters to the floor, someone knocks over their chair, and teachers yell for everyone else to *stop* yelling, which only adds to the nuttiness.

"It's not the zombie apocalypse, people!" Macy shouts, but no one can hear her over the noise except for me.

I hold my arms out straight in front of me and sway from side to side and stick my tongue out like I'm a zombie. Which probably doesn't help to make things less chaotic, but it at least makes Macy laugh.

The lights come back on by the end of lunch, but it's like everyone is buzzing and electrified for the rest of the day. Even on the bus everyone is extra loud and the ride extra bumpy. The bus driver yells, "Quiet down!" just about every other minute.

On our walk to the corner, I actually welcome the quiet between Macy and me. As we part ways, Macy says, "See you tomorrow," and then she does something that surprises me: she gives me a hug. The last time someone other than my moms or Gramps hugged me was when I was saying goodbye to Jude on the morning she left.

"See you tomorrow!" I hug her back. "And tell your grandma I said hi!"

"I will!" Macy says, waving as she walks away.

**✳ ✳ ✳**

**I jog the** rest of the way home so I can see Dewey sooner. I stop short at the end of my driveway, when I see that Mama's car is parked there.

"I'm home," I say as I step inside and remove my coat and boots.

Gramps is sitting on the couch with a book. He turns to look at me and sort of winks, then gives me the *okay* sign and points out the window toward the shed. I take that to mean everything is in order and Dewey is safe in her Puppy Palace.

I silently nod in return, mouthing the words, *Thank you.*

"Sadie, I'm in here!" Mama shouts back.

I make my way into the kitchen and see that Mama is slicing up a block of cheese, the kind with the spicy peppers that I love.

"Hungry?" she asks. "Cheese and crackers."

It's not PB&J, but I am hungry. Things got so wild in the cafeteria that almost nobody finished their lunch today, including me. I steal a piece of cheese and take a bite while I sit down at the table. "How'd you get home before me today, anyway?" I ask Mama.

Noah comes down the stairs, like he can sense that

254

there's food, and he immediately swoops in to grab a handful of cheese and crackers from the plate.

"Things were hectic today with the weather," Mama groans. "Nobody was staying late, so I decided to give myself a little break and come home to see you guys." She looks up from the cutting board. "Well, don't look so happy to see me," she jokes.

"Oh, right. I am," I tell her, even though that's a lie.

Her being here means I won't be able to see Dewey. My stomach suddenly feels so swimmy and nervous, I can barely swallow the bite of cheese I've been chewing.

Next, as if my anxiety wasn't already steadily rising, the front door opens and we hear Mom come in. "Hello, my loves," she calls out.

"Hey," Mama says, standing up to give Mom a kiss on the cheek. "You're home early too?"

"My last appointment got canceled 'cause of this storm that's coming in, so"—she raises her arms out to the sides—"here I am!"

Terrific.

I twitch my head to the side and widen my eyes, trying to give Gramps a silent message—*We need to talk!* But it's Noah who picks up on it.

"What's that about?" he asks, imitating my head twitch.

"Nothing, just stretching." I shake my shoulders out

and turn my head from side to side. Noah makes a face and walks away.

"*Psst*, Gramps." I tug on his sleeve and lead him into the hall. "What are we going to do?"

He shrugs. "Not much we *can* do."

"She can't stay out there by herself in this storm," I whisper. "It's only going to get worse."

"She'll be okay, Sass."

"No, she won't," I argue. I wish everyone would stop saying that things are going to be okay. "Maybe now is the time?"

He squints like he's not sure what I mean.

"To tell Moms about Dewey," I explain. "They're not going to make her stay out in the rain by herself. This is probably the best chance we're going to get."

"No"—he shakes his head fiercely—"not yet."

"But Gramps—"

"Sass, what did I say?" His voice is stern, but not quite yelling. "Not. Now."

"Hey," Mom appears in the kitchen doorway, looking back and forth between us. "What's going on with you two?"

Gramps raises his eyebrows and gives me the tiniest headshake so that Mom can't see. "*Don't*," he whispers under his breath, widening his eyes at me.

I'm willing to risk the wrath of my moms if it means Dewey won't have to spend another scared night outside, but as I look into Gramps's eyes, I get a little scared of this new wrath of *his* I never knew existed before the other night.

I look back and forth between them, and I clench my jaw muscles so hard my back molars ache. "Nothing," I finally mutter. But it isn't nothing. It's a lot of things: it's Dewey being stuck in the storm; it's me telling Moms another load of applesauce; it's me worrying if Gramps will be mad. It's too much.

I storm upstairs to my room, slamming the door behind me. Inside, I feel my own wrath churning up inside of me, and I don't know who I'm angrier at: me or Gramps. I throw myself onto my bed and smother my face into my pillow. I want to shout into it again, but when I open my mouth it's not a scream this time; it's a wail. Angry tears fall hot and fast, absorbing into the fabric.

There's a knock on my door.

I blubber, "Go away!" But when I pull my face from the pillow, Noah is standing in my doorway.

"What's with you?" he asks, looking at me with his face all scrunched up like he's actually concerned.

"Like you really care," I snort, swiping my sleeve across my wet eyes.

"Try me," he says, holding his hands up in front of him as he steps inside my room. "Come on, what? Are you in a fight with your friend or something?"

"Yeah." I sniffle. "Sort of." I *am* technically fighting with Jude, but the person I really want to be talking with Noah about right now is *Gramps*.

Noah takes a seat in my desk chair and says, "I've gotten into plenty of arguments with my friends before, so I'm sure I have lots of older-sibling wisdom on the subject." He grins and stifles a laugh, adding, "I mean, if you wanna tell me about it."

"Well, what would you do if someone you care about is not making the smartest decisions?" I ask.

"About what?"

"Just stuff," I answer. Noah stares, waiting for more information, so I continue, "Okay, let's just say this person is not being completely honest to their . . . *parents* . . . about something. And I don't know if I should tell on them or not."

"Depends. Are they not being honest about something that could get them hurt?"

"No."

He raises an eyebrow. "Something illegal?"

I laugh. "No, nothing illegal."

"So, why are you so upset about it, then?"

"Because it's not like I'm just keeping a secret; it's like I'm lying too."

Noah squints, staring into the distance, thinking. "Then I don't know. Maybe I'm not all that much older and wiser after all." He sighs. "Okay, my best advice: If you have to tell, *tell*. But try not to judge Jude, you know?" he adds. "It can't be easy being in a new place."

Surprisingly, Noah may not be quite as big of a butt-head as I thought. He's actually managed to make me feel better about both Gramps *and* Jude.

As soon as Noah leaves my room, there's a rumble of thunder that growls in the distance. Which brings me back to the true source of why I'm mad at Gramps: Dewey. None of Noah's wisdom can help me feel better about Dewey being stuck outside, alone, right now. This storm is only getting closer.


**I don't say** much to anyone at dinner, especially Gramps. And when I go upstairs to my room afterward, I flip through my homework assignments, but I can't stop worrying about Dewey.

Once I'm in bed, every time I almost fall asleep there's another roll of thunder that wakes me up. "I'm here, Dewey," I whisper, but I don't hear her respond in my thoughts.

The next thing I know, I'm awoken by a crack of lightning that illuminates my entire room, followed by the kind of thunder that sounds so close it might split my house in half. I check my clock: it's the middle of the night.

The rain is pounding against my window so hard I actually feel a little scared it might break the glass. But worse than that, underneath all the noise I hear the most desperate, lonely howl.

I shoot out of bed and down the stairs without even thinking, because all my insides are shaking with fear—but not *mine*. It's Dewey's. With my bathrobe draped over my head, I run out to the shed and fling open the door. I don't even see her at first. She's hiding. A trembling ball under Mama's worktable. I kneel down and open my arms, and Dewey scrambles over to me.

Even though she's half my size, I gather her up in my arms like a baby, and she clings to me with her paws tight around my shoulders. I cover us both with my bathrobe and run toward the house. I don't know how I find the strength, but I do. I carry her all the way up the stairs and into my bedroom. She never stops shivering. I finally set her down on the rug and sit there holding her until she calms down.

Her thoughts are frantic, jumping back and forth between now and her old memories of the house with the mean people.

"You're okay. I'm here. I'm not leaving you alone."

I tell her that over and over. Until her thoughts begin to slow and stay with me in the present. "You're sleeping in a real bed tonight, where you belong," I whisper.

She follows me to my bed, and I pull the covers up over us, still holding on to her tight. I don't fall asleep until I hear the sound of her steady breathing, in and out, letting me know she's finally resting. I kiss her head, and close my eyes too.

## Chapter 29

# THE BEST DAY

My alarm clock is buzzing like a swarm of bees around my head. Without opening my eyes, I reach from under the warmth of my blanket and sweep my arm across the nightstand until my hand finds that stupid rectangular noise machine. I slam it until there's silence.

Groaning, I pull the covers over my head, burying my face in my pillow.

Then my pillow moves. Wet breath on my face. Licking. Dewey!

My eyes fly open. We are face-to-face, her head next to me on my pillow. She yawns and whines, groggily looking around my room.

*Let's stay here all day.*

"I would love that, Dewey, but—"

There's a knock on my door, and Mama sticks her head in, saying, "Sadie, you awake?"

I throw the blanket over Dewey. "I'm up, Mama."

She starts to close the door, but looks up. I'm positive she's staring at the giant dog-shaped lump next to me. "Are you okay?"

"I—"

Now Mom comes in. "Are you getting ready for school?"

They both stand there, watching me, waiting for an answer.

"Moms, I—" I pause, uncertain of what is going to happen. I tell Dewey, with all my brainpower, *Don't move.* "I don't feel good."

Mama walks over to my bedside; I pull the blankets tight. She feels my forehead, then my cheeks. "Goodness, you're warm."

I *am* warm. But not because I'm sick—I have a doggy-sized furnace lying in bed right next to me.

"Well, I think I know what's going on," Mom says, crossing her arms. This is it. I'm caught. No way she's buying this; she's going to say I'm faking. She's going to tell me to get out of bed right this instant and—

"You caught yourself a cold from running around in the rain." She shakes her head and points her finger at me. "Let this be a lesson, Sadie. I'll tell Gramps you're staying home."

Mama leans down and smooths my hair back, saying, "Feel better, honey."

"You get lots of rest," Mom adds, and kisses my forehead.

"Okay," I whisper.

They leave my room and close the door, but Dewey and I stay still under the blankets for the whole forty-three minutes it takes them to finish getting ready and leave the house. When I hear cars pulling out of the driveway, I throw the covers off and go to the window.

They're gone.

Dewey is sitting up in bed, ears twitching as she listens to the fading engines. She jumps down and does a full-body shake to get her excitement out.

We start the day with Dewey chasing her ball, running around the yard faster and freer than ever before. After I explain everything that happened with the storm last night, Gramps says he supposes she can stay in today, since it's cold out.

"But just for today," he adds.

I don't want to argue with him, so I don't mention telling Moms again, but I'm going to have to soon. I bring Dewey's food and water bowl and bed in from the shed, and she eats breakfast with Catniss in the kitchen. Dewey says food tastes better with company, and I believe her. After they finish, Catniss inspects Dewey's bed and rolls around in it, meowing loudly and endlessly, until Dewey comes over and curls up around her.

Gramps and I bring cold pizza to the couch and turn on Cartoon Central while Dewey and Catniss nap. Gramps nods off next. I close my eyes, but I don't doze. I know why. There's something I need to do.

Quietly, I go upstairs to my bedroom and open my laptop.

Monday

JUDE: Helllloooooo? Are you not getting these messages?

JUDE: I even tried calling you twice! Jordie held my hand after school today while we walked home!!!

JUDE: Omg! it was weird and nice, idk how to describe it . . . my palms were all sweaty which sounds gross but it really wasn't

JUDE: lemme know when you can talk

Tuesday

JUDE: What is going on???? I have major major major news. Big developments happening all over the place

JUDE: Also, dad said I can visit for code name: winter break!

Wednesday

JUDE: Please call AS SOON AS you get this

Thursday

JUDE: what the crap, Sadie?!

Friday

JUDE: I'm about to leave for school. I need to know if you still want me to come for winter break.

JUDE: jordie asked me to the snowflake ball (it's a dance thing that I'm sure you think is stupid). it happens over winter break and I can't give them an answer until I hear from you!

JUDE: just so you know I'm mad at you

*Crap.* My hands are on the keyboard, and even though there are so many things I want to say, I can't make my fingers tap out the right words.

ME: Jude, I'm sorry. I have been so busy with Dewey I haven't been paying attention to my messages.

But that's not the whole truth. I delete it and try again.

ME: of course i still want you to come. but only if you do too. So much has happened with gramps and dewey and even macy, and i feel like you don't care. Lately it seems like we have less and less in common.

I can't say that either, though. I delete it.

ME: I don't know if I want you to come anymore.
Because what if you do and then all you want is
to go home and be with your new firends?

ME: *friends

No. Delete, delete!

ME: I'm sorry you're upset with me
but I'm mad at you too!

That's the one I send. My words sit there staring back
at me, all mean and selfish and not explaining anything.
But I can't take them back now. I start typing to explain,
but Gramps is calling me downstairs.

"One minute, Gramps," I yell back.

"No, Sadie," he says. "Come now."

There's something serious in his tone. Plus, he called
me *Sadie*.

I abandon my explanation and race down the stairs,
yelling, "Gramps, what's wrong?" But he doesn't need to
answer, because I see what's wrong, and my heart drops
all the way into my stomach.

## Chapter 30

# THE PIZZA HITS THE FLOOR (CHEESE SIDE DOWN)

Mama is standing in the living room holding a plastic bag filled with takeout. "I thought I'd bring you soup on my lunch break, seeing as you were feeling so sick this morning."

Dewey is sitting in her bed, watching Mama. *Oh no*, Dewey thinks, and lets out a little whimper.

Mama sets the food on the kitchen table and says, in her firm teacher voice, "So does anyone care to explain to me why there is a dog in our living room?"

"Mama, I—"

"Wait." Gramps holds his hand up. "Let me explain."

Gramps spills the whole story, except the way he tells it makes it sound more like it was *my* idea. And I wonder if he's trying to blame me or if that's really how he remembers it. My face gets hot, and I feel mad and sad all at once.

Mama listens, and when he finishes with how Dewey ended up in my bed this morning, she doesn't say anything. She goes to the cupboard and takes down three bowls and spoons and begins unpacking the takeout.

"So we have wonton, egg drop, and hot and sour," she says.

"But, Mama—" I begin.

She stops me. "I need to think, Sadie. Eating helps me think."

I'm silent as I watch Mama pour herself a bowl of hot and sour soup—her favorite.

I sit on the floor next to Dewey's bed. She shifts and sits in my lap, her poor foxtail shivering.

*I'm scared. Do I have to leave?*

"It's okay," I whisper. "It's going to be okay."

Only I don't know that for sure, so of course Dewey can tell.

Gramps lets out a long sigh as he joins Mama at the table, and pours himself some egg drop. They both start eating, and the only noise in the entire house is the sound of spoons scraping bowls, followed by an occasional slurp.

At last, I hear Mama's chair legs scrape against the floor, and she walks toward me. Neither Dewey nor I can look her in the eye. She sits on the couch and holds her hand out to Dewey.

"C'mere, you," Mama says softly.

Dewey raises her head and sniffs Mama's hand, then lets her pet her head and ears, leaning into Mama's touch.

"Sadie, what do you have to say about all this?" Mama finally asks me.

"I lied, I know. But it's not like I didn't *want* to tell you the truth."

Mama looks at Gramps, then back to me. "Why don't you go to your room for now? You can take the dog." She pulls out her phone. "I have to call Mom."

"Wait, what are you going to tell her?"

"The truth." Mama has the phone pressed to her ear, waiting for Mom to pick up. "We always tell the truth, Sadie—that's how this family works."

I stand up, but I don't go to my room. I look back and forth between Mama and Gramps and Dewey, thinking about how we got here in the first place. *We do not always tell the truth in this family*—I want to shout it.

"Yeah, Katie," Mama says into the phone. "You need to come home—the pizza's really hit the floor here, babe," she says under her breath.

We all sit in our separate corners, giving each other the silent treatment until Mom gets home. At first, Mama and Gramps begin to explain the whole story, but as soon as they get past the basics, Mom interrupts, "What. Were. You. *Thinking?*" Mom's voice seems to get louder with each word. She's looking at me, but she's looking at Gramps too.

"Dewey needed us," I tell her. "And you just wouldn't listen to me, Moms—both of you."

Gramps raises his voice now. "I was thinking I wanted to do something nice for my daughter! What is so wrong with that?"

"Your *daughter?*" Mom repeats.

"You know what I mean—my *granddaughter!*"

Now everyone is talking at the same time, nobody listening to each other at all. I cover my ears and close my eyes tight, letting my head rest against Dewey's. This wasn't supposed to happen—they were supposed to find out later, once we figured out a way to tell them.

*Is it my fault?*

"No. I promise it's not your fault," I whisper to Dewey, not caring if anyone else hears me.

"You should've known better, Dad!" Mom says. "I trusted you here. You know we've been trying so hard to get Sadie on track—you have totally undermined us, not to mention that you've put her in danger."

"Now, that is just not true, Katie!" Gramps points his finger at Mom. "I would never!"

"But you did!" Mom shouts. "You have put us all in danger."

"Nonsense—the dog is perfectly tame, Katie. *You* should know better," he shouts, turning Mom's own words back on her.

"Dad, you could've burned the house down the other night!"

Gramps shakes his head. "There it is." He laughs, waving his arm in Mom's direction. "Out with it, then—what do you think, I'm off my noggin just because of a little accident?"

"It was not a small thing, Ed," Mama says, then turns to me. "Sadie, it's really time for you to go upstairs."

"*No!*" I shout. "Just stop! I'm not going to my room— you two always do that. You're so angry about me and Gramps keeping this big secret, but that's what you guys do all the time!"

"You lower your voice right this min—" but I interrupt her.

"You and Mama didn't tell the truth about Gramps. I mean, why he's *really* here. I'm not a baby anymore, you know."

"So, this is all somehow my and your mother's fault now?" Mom asks. "How do you figure that?"

"No, it's not. I'm just saying . . . maybe if you trusted me with the truth in the first place, I wouldn't have to keep any secrets at all!"

"What was I supposed to say?" Mom's voice is scratchy, and I can see the tears flooding her eyes. She turns to Mama now too, like she's asking her as well. "That Gramps has dementia? That he's getting worse all the time? That"—her voice breaks now, and she lowers herself to the couch—"that I don't know how to take care of him? Is that what I was supposed to tell you?"

"Katie!" Gramps scolds. "That's applesauce—"

"No, Dad, it's true," she says sadly. "And the fact that you let Sadie talk you into this whole dog thing proves it—you're not thinking clearly."

"She didn't talk me into it!" he shouts. "I talked her in . . . to . . ." His voice drifts off, and as he realizes what he's saying, his face goes blank, his shoulders slope in, and I can barely hear the last word: "*It.*"

Gramps turns the weight of his gaze onto me now, and he opens his mouth like he's about to speak, but it takes longer for his brain to find the words. "Why couldn't you just stick to the plan?" he asks, his voice brittle and rough with sadness now, instead of anger.

I can't answer him. I wish I could've stuck to the plan for him a little longer. "I'm sorry!" I manage to whimper as I run out of the room and up the stairs, Dewey on my heels.

I throw myself onto my bed. Dewey nuzzles her face into mine, trying to make me feel better, when really, I should be the one comforting *her*. All the yelling is still echoing in my head. So is that word . . . *dementia*. It keeps repeating, and I know for sure that Gramps is not okay. I can't hold it in anymore. I sob. I sob the way I did the day Jude left. Dewey licks my tears.

*I could run away.*

"What!" I say out loud. "No! Don't even think that."

*It would be hard, especially now that I know.*

"Know what?" I ask her.

*What it's like to have a home.*

"I'm not going to let that happen. Moms are angry, but I know I can talk to them. Dewey, the fight wasn't really about you."

*It seemed like it was.*

"Once Mom meets you—really meets you and sees how amazing you are—I know she'll change her mind. But no growling."

*As long as there are no cages.*

"We don't do cages here."

We snuggle up together in my bed. Dewey falls asleep, but not me. I stare at the ceiling. The house is totally quiet now, and I hear a *bloopbloop* sound come from my laptop, which means Jude must have gotten home from school by now and seen my message.

Not long after, I hear footsteps in the hallway. I open

my eyes; I must have fallen asleep. Dewey stirs in my arms and looks toward the door.

*Knock, knock.* "It's me," Noah mumbles.

"Come in," I say, hoping it's nice Noah and not butt-head Noah tonight.

The door opens, and Catniss slinks inside and leaps onto my bed. Noah sets his backpack down in the hall and steps inside too. I wait for him to tell me how badly I screwed up.

When he opens his mouth, though, he *laughs.* "So I guess you're pretty much grounded for life, huh?" It's not that it's funny, this situation, but his jokey tone gives me permission to smile, like maybe it will be okay someday, even if it's not okay today.

"Moms told you everything?"

He nods and reaches out his hand for Dewey to sniff, and then pats her head. "It's about time we had a dog around here, if you ask me." He starts to get comfortable, rubbing Dewey under the chin. But then he stops abruptly and looks all around my room. "Wait a minute, where's Gramps? Mom told me to come up here and ask you guys to come downstairs."

"Gramps hasn't been up here all day," I answer.

## Chapter 31

# MISSING

Noah and I check all the rooms upstairs. We race to the kitchen to tell Moms. Dewey and Catniss follow along behind us like they're our shadows.

Mom and Mama are in the living room sitting together on the couch.

They stand up when they see us without Gramps.

"Where is he?" Mom whispers, reaching out for Mama's hand.

"We will find him," Mama says firmly, snapping into action. "Noah, check the front yard. Sadie, you go out back. I'll start calling the neighbors."

Dewey runs outside with me. We check the shed. The gate is still latched. I even inspect the crumbling fairy fortress for any signs or clues he may have left me.

"Gramps?" I yell.

Nothing.

Inside, Moms are getting their coats and shoes on.

"Where are you going?" Noah asks, clearly not having had any luck in the front yard either.

"We're going to drive around and look for him," Mama explains. "He can't have gotten far."

Mom wipes her eyes and sniffles. "You two stay here in case he comes back. And keep your phones close," she tells both Noah and me. They rush out the door, leaving us behind.

Gramps is missing. I have to do something. I can't just stay here and wait. "Think," I whisper. "Think, Sadie."

*The spot.* I look at Dewey. *The special spot.*

"Oh my gosh, Dewey, you're right!" I start putting on my sneakers and my coat—I don't even bother to get changed out of the pajamas I've been wearing all day.

"Sadie, what do you think you're doing?" Noah says, blocking the back door as I clip Dewey's leash onto her collar. "Moms said to stay here."

"But I think I know where he is," I tell Noah. "There's this spot in the woods that he really likes."

"You know you're not supposed to go out there by yourself."

"I'll take Dewey—I know exactly where I'm going, and I'll be careful, and if I'm right, then I'll be coming home with Gramps." I wait for his response. "Trust me," I add. "Please?"

He hesitates, weighing our options, of which we have few. Then he looks at Dewey, and finally sighs. "Okay, but I'm coming. And we have to hurry—it's going to be getting dark soon."

Armed with my coat, scarf, boots, and Dewey and Noah, we pass the clearing where Dewey and I first met, and I march ahead, clear on my mission. Farther along the trail, I close my eyes remembering the way Gramps was looking at all the trees along the path, and I smile, knowing that I'm going to run into him at any moment now.

"He'll be there," I assure Noah.

One strange thing I notice is that I don't see any birds or squirrels, rabbits or toads, even though I know they're here somewhere. It's like the woods have lost their magic. I take the path all the way to the pond. But when I get there, it's deserted. I was sure he'd be here waiting for me. I circle the entire pond, walking along the edge of the water, my boots punching through the underbrush into holes and soft spots in the earth. Dewey sniffs alongside me.

I cup my hands around my mouth and yell, as loud as I can, "Gramps?"

I call out again, and I can see from the corner of my eye, Noah is checking his phone, his eyes crinkled with worry. Dewey howls—a siren call to Gramps. I sit down on the broken tree stump, and I close my eyes, concentrate on my thoughts, and try, with everything I have, to tell Gramps, *Please come home.*

**Noah finally gets** me to believe Gramps isn't coming, and we run the whole way back to beat the sunset. Noah sits at the counter and runs his hands through his damp hair. The quiet is sticky and cold. I feel myself shaking. "I thought for sure he'd be there, Noah—I'm really getting worried now."

"I know; so am I." Noah sounds scared too, which makes me even more scared.

A car door slams, and Mom walks in.

"Did you find him?" I shout.

Mom shakes her head. "Mama dropped me off. She's going to keep driving around looking for him. I've got to start making some more calls. It's getting darker and colder out there."

I pace back and forth across the living room, while Mom makes phone calls to hospitals and Gramps's old neighbors in his apartment building and even Macy's father, asking if anyone has seen him.

Dinnertime comes and goes. And still nothing.

"Mom?" I whisper, joining her at the kitchen table

where she's been scribbling notes on a pad of paper. "I'm really sorry."

She cuts her eyes to me and sighs. "I know." But what I really want her to say is, "It's okay," or "It's going to be okay," or "It's not your fault."

I try again. "I never meant for any of this to happen."

"I know," she repeats, more firmly, focusing on her notepad so hard she won't even look at me.

"Mom, I feel terrible," I add.

She slams her pen down on the pad of paper. "Sadie, please!" she shouts. "I know you're sorry. I know you feel terrible, but—I can't—I have to focus on this right now. I don't have time to"—she pauses, picks up the pen, and, under her breath, mutters—"*make you feel better.*"

My chin quivers, but I try to be strong and suck my tears back up. I want to say so much more, but I don't have a chance because the phone rings.

Both Mom and I jump. Noah races into the room.

Mom answers by the second ring. "Dad?" Silence. "Oh, I'm sorry . . . uh, yes. Yes, that's him. He was? But he's not hurt? Oh, thank goodness," she says. "Yes. Absolutely. I'm on my way right now—thank you. Thank you so much."

She sets her phone down and immediately hangs her head in her hands and bursts out crying.

"Mom, what is it?" Noah asks.

Mom nods as she catches her breath. "He's okay," she tells us.

Noah and I look at each other, relieved, while Mom dials the phone again.

"Elle—yes, he's all right. Yeah. He's at the police station downtown—they picked him up, trying to get on a bus to the city without a ticket," she explains. "Okay, okay, I'll be waiting."

"He's at the police station?" I ask. "Is he in trouble?"

"He's not in trouble. He's just confused and—" Mom stops herself, pulls in a deep gulp of air before continuing. "I mean, he's *not* just confused. He had one of his episodes again. But he's safe; that's the important thing."

**Mama picks Mom** up to go to the police station. Noah is on the phone with Kendra, telling her about everything that's happened.

So I take Dewey to my room.

I close the door and slump down onto my floor like a limp balloon animal, Dewey leaning against me. I should feel better now, knowing that Gramps is safe. But it's the opposite. Now that the worry is gone, it's made room for other things. Like whether Gramps will forgive me for breaking our secret, or Dewey's uncertain fate. Like whether things with Jude will ever be normal again, or the way Mom snapped at me tonight. It's that last one that's sticking its thorns in me now. And not only because she kind of hurt my feelings, but because somewhere deep down, I know that she was right.

I can't always wait for someone else to make me feel better, or get lost in a daydream until the murky feelings subside. Sometimes, I guess I should be responsible for making myself feel better. But I can't solve all my problems at once; I have to tackle one thing at a time, like Moms are always telling me.

I look at Dewey; she blinks her soft, wet eyes at me.

"I know what I need to do," I tell her. "First things first."

I sit down at my desk, and I type out everything in messages that are pages and pages long. Everything I've tried to tell Jude, everything about Gramps and Dewey and my IEP, and everything I've wanted to say and haven't, and even some things I didn't realize until now. I finish off with what I think is a good thing to tell her:

> ME: So I guess maybe I've also been a little jealous of your new friends (even jordie) and it was easier to just stop listening to you than to think that we're growing apart.

> ME: I should've been more honest about how I was feeling.

ME: But I guess the real reason for everything is that I miss you, and I hate when things change, but I know nothing can just stay the same forever (that would be boring!)

ME: p.s. i would be soooo happy if you could still come for winter break. and if you do, I really want you and macy to be friends too because she's pretty terrific! please think about it, biffle <3

There's a knock on my bedroom door. It's Noah. "Whatcha doing?" he asks. "Wanna hang out?"

"Are you just being nice to me because you know I feel like crap right now?" I ask.

He makes a *pshh* sound and says, "No. Why would I do that?" he retorts. "Also, don't say *crap*."

Downstairs, Noah makes us a bag of microwave popcorn and we play video games while he shows me all the secret maneuvers it's taken him years to perfect. It helps the time go by faster, and I realize I am starting to feel just a little bit better.

Dewey and Catniss curl up between us on the couch, each of them snoring in an alternating rhythm, blocking out the crashing and banging sounds of the video game. It's almost ten o'clock before we hear the car pull into the driveway. Dewey barks once, announcing their return.

Noah and I rush to the front door, watching them

come up the walkway with Gramps. When they get inside, everyone looks ragged and exhausted. Gramps is wearing a coat I don't recognize—I guess they must've given it to him at the police station.

He blinks a few times like he's waking up from a dream and is seeing us for the first time. "Hiya, kids," he says. His voice is so quiet.

"Are you okay, Gramps?" I ask.

He looks at me, but he doesn't answer.

Instead, Mama says, "We'll talk about everything in the morning, but for now let's get everyone to bed."

Noah and I say our goodnights and head upstairs, while Mom helps Gramps to get out of his coat. At the top of the stairs, Noah starts to head down the hall to his room.

"Noah?" I say, and he turns around. "Thanks."

I don't have to say what for—Noah knows—he smiles and mumbles, "G'night, dork."

# Chapter 32

# CHAMOMILE AND HONEY

Even though Gramps is back, it's hard to fall asleep. I still feel like I need to *do* something. I think again about what Mom said to me earlier. I know it's not her job to make me feel better, but maybe I can do something to make *her* feel better instead.

I creep downstairs, Dewey following along behind me. But Mom and Mama are already sitting at the kitchen table, the pamphlets from their bedroom now neatly folded and fanned out across the table like a deck of cards.

"Hi," I say quietly as I enter the room, and they both look up from the table.

"What are you doing awake?" Mom asks me.

"I was going to make some tea for you." I reach for the new kettle that has replaced the old burned-up one. "Chamomile with honey?"

Mom's face softens. "That sounds nice."

While I wait for the water to boil, I take their two

favorite mugs out of the cupboard—the ones that say *Mrs.* and *Mrs.*—and prepare them each with a teabag, the string carefully wrapped around the handle, the jar of honey opened and ready to be added.

I sit down at the table and take a deep breath, in then out, and say, "I am sorry, Moms—and I'm not just saying that so you'll tell me it's okay. I know it's not. I know this is all my fault."

"Look at me." Mom reaches out and holds my face steady in her soft hands, her red-rimmed eyes meeting mine. "What happened with Gramps today—that is *not* your fault."

I nod and try to believe her.

"But don't think that means we're not still extremely upset with you about the lying," she says, pressing her lips into a firm line.

Mama nods in agreement and adds, "You knew better than to pull something like this, Sade," gesturing to Dewey, who is looking back and forth between each of us.

"I know." I look down at my lap and Dewey comes over and pushes her head into my hand. "You should ground me until high school," I offer.

"Oh, I can think of something much more fitting than that," Mom replies, with a hint of something like her mischievous board-game laugh vibrating under her words.

Just then, the kettle begins building its high-pitched

scream, so I get up and quickly remove it from the stove, pour the water into the *Mrs.* mugs, and finally spoon in big globs of honey. I bring the cups to the table and carefully set them down without spilling.

"Thank you," Mama tells me.

Mom leans over and looks at Dewey in this thoughtful way, and I wonder if they're telepathically communicating and I just can't hear it. She smooths her hands over Dewey's head and ears, giving her a big pat on her flank. Dewey rests her chin on Mom's knee and looks up at her with those warm puppy eyes full of love and comfort.

Mom glances at Mama, and they share one of their *looks*.

"Oh, fine," Mom mumbles to Dewey. She rolls her eyes, and with a lopsided smile forming on her face, she says, "You can stay."

"Really?" I squeak. Dewey's ears perk up, and her tail swishes back and forth. "Did you hear that?" I tell her. "You're really home now—your *forever* home."

Dewey runs over to where Catniss is curled up on the couch and wakes her up like she's telling her the good news.

"Moms, thank you! I can't even—I just—thank you."

"All right, all right," Mama says as I throw my arms around each of them, kissing their cheeks. "It's still the middle of the night, and you need to get to bed."

"Punishment forthcoming," Mom calls after me as I make my way upstairs.

Dewey follows me into my bedroom, and as I close the door behind us, I let out a huge sigh of relief. I sit down at my desk and take my slippers off, and that's when I see the blinking message icon on my laptop.

JUDE: thx for telling me the truth. I'm still kind of mad but maybe we can talk more this weekend?

JUDE: By the way, I still really miss you too.

I look down at Dewey, curled up at my feet, and even though *so* much has gone wrong these past few days, somehow things feel like they happened just the way they were supposed to. I try to remember that word Gramps had said when we were in Patrick's car, the thing that happens when a little luck and a little magic come together.

I close out my messages window and I open Definasaurus.com. I start typing. Autocorrect tries to change it to "saran wrap" and "serenity" and "serenade" but I finally get it right: *serendipity.*

ser·en·dip·i·ty /ser-ən-'di-pə-tē/

noun: *serendipity*; plural: *serendipities*

1. the occurrence and development of events by chance in a happy or beneficial way.

2. good fortune; luck.

3. an aptitude for making desirable discoveries by accident.

I close my laptop and get myself all tucked in. I pat the side of the bed for Dewey to jump up. "Come on, girl," I tell her. She jumps on the bed and sits across from me, looking around the room, panting with her doggy smile. "You ready for bed?"

She flops over on her back for belly rubs.

"You're so silly."

She paws at my hand so I will keep petting her, and whines and kisses my fingers. "Why are you being so quiet, huh?"

She blinks her big soft eyes at me, but doesn't respond. "Dewey?" I say, louder.

But the only thoughts in my head are my own.

"Serendipity?" I call her instead.

With that, she stands up and turns around in circles, barking once as she play-bows at me. "Serendipity," I repeat, and she barks again. "That's your new name, isn't it?"

She kisses my hand and looks up at me in that loving way she always has, except something has changed. Somehow, I know she won't be talking to me anymore— at least not the way she did.

## Chapter 33

# FRENCH TOAST WITH A SIDE OF SERENDIPITY

It's been one month since Gramps moved to Oakwood Village. I carry a shopping bag on each arm, along with Serendipity's leash wrapped around my wrist, and hold the elevator while I wait for Mom and Mama and Noah to catch up to us.

When they do, the door closes with a sharp *ping*.

I press the *3* button, and up we go. The elevator lets out on Gramps's floor, and we step out into the hallway. Mrs. Santiago is there, waiting to get on.

"Hello, Serendipity," she says. She balances herself with her cane as she bends over to pet Serendipity's head. "I don't have any cookies for you today."

We pass the doors of Gramps's new neighbors on the left and right, and at the end of the hall is Gramps's apartment, with his name on a plaque next to his door that reads EDWIN MITCHELL.

We knock, but the door is already cracked open.

"Hello?" Mom calls as we walk in.

"Come on in!" Gramps shouts.

He's gotten a lot of unpacking done since we were here last weekend. Now there's even a small Chrismukkah tree sitting on the coffee table.

"Wow, Ed," Mama says. "Where'd the tree come from?"

He comes out of the kitchen, wiping his hands on a dish towel. He pulls me into a hug as he takes the grocery bags from my hands. "Toshi brought it for me."

"Macy's grandma came to visit you?" I ask, surprised.

"Yes, I happen to be a very popular person," Gramps jokes.

This apartment is different from his last one: It's smaller but newer. It's closer to our house. He has a balcony that overlooks a garden. And here, he has a list on his wall with important phone numbers, like ours, like the front desk's, even his own. Next to the door is a checklist he made himself, so he doesn't forget to do anything important before he leaves his apartment:

1. *lock door*

2. *check stove*

3. *keys*

4. *wallet*

5. *phone*

"Serendipity," Gramps calls for her, and pats his hands against his legs. "Come here, girl!" She does a circle in front of him and sits down for Gramps to give her head rubs. She raises her face, her nose wiggling as she sniffs the air, wagging her tail, following her nose into the kitchen.

"Now, don't worry," Gramps says, "I'm cooking faken *and* the real stuff for the carnivores."

"Hear! Hear!" Noah says, raising his hand.

I follow the scent as well. I hear humming coming from behind the open refrigerator door. Then Mom stands up, and I can see that she is holding a carton of eggs in one hand and milk in the other, and wax paper-wrapped butter in the crook of her arm. She closes the fridge door with her foot as she turns toward the counter.

"Am I dreaming, or are we having French toast?"

Mom throws her head back and laughs—and for just a second I see it: the resemblance to Grandma in the picture Gramps now keeps on his nightstand.

"You're not dreaming," she tells me.

Mama comes in the kitchen then and says, quietly, "Why don't you and Serendipity go and give Gramps his gift now?" She hands me the box I wrapped last night in my bedroom with the comics pages from the newspaper. "Breakfast will be ready soon."

Serendipity jumps up on the couch and curls into

a ball. Gramps is sitting in his favorite chair, which we brought from his old apartment.

"Look at that," Gramps says, hitching his chin in the direction of Serendipity. "She's at home already, isn't she?"

"Yep," I say, sitting down next to him. "How about you?"

"Me?" He rocks his hand from side to side like a seesaw. "Well, I'm getting there."

"Good," I say, and then I pull out the box from behind my back and hold it out to him.

"Sassafras!" he says, smiling big and bright as he turns to me. "What do you have there?"

"It's an early Chrismukkah gift for you," I tell him. "From me and Serendipity."

Gramps smiles as he carefully unties the string and unwraps the box. He pulls off the lid and removes all the tissue paper, and gasps. "Did you finish?"

I nod. "I wanted to get it done before Jude gets here, because then I would've had to wait a whole other week to give it to you."

"Gee," he sings, as he examines the cover.

"Look at what it says on the inside," I tell him.

He reads, "*The Interstellar Adventures of S. Hawkins, Special Agent* by Sadie Kathryn Eleanor Mitchell-Rosen."

"After that," I tell him, "on the next page."

He turns the page carefully, and I can see him reading

the words to himself first. He looks up at me then, his eyes all misty, but he clears his throat and continues, "For Edwin Mitchell, the best Gramps in the world."

I wanted him to have those words in writing so even if he forgets, he'll always have something to remind him. It took a lot of hard work to finish S. Hawkins's story—especially between my daily after-school Doodie Duty punishment and helping to convert the She Shed back into Mama's studio, and not missing a single homework assignment this entire past month—but I did it.


**It's funny how** not so long ago all I wanted was for things to go back to the way they were. Now I'm starting to think that not all changes are bad. If things never changed, then Gramps wouldn't be here at Oakwood Village where he needs to be. Noah wouldn't have had a chance to become less buttheaded. Macy and I wouldn't even be friends. And I never would've met Serendipity, the one who made everything change for the better.

I won't spoil the ending for Gramps, but I decided that I would make S. Hawkins have some fragments of her memories return to her, along with some that never do, but she realizes that her new mission isn't to climb the mountain in order to find a way *off* Earth; it's to figure out how to stay here, to find out what happens next.

It's sort of like that with me too. A month ago, I didn't know what the puzzle of my life was going to look like. But somehow all the right pieces found their way into the picture at the right moment. Serendipity was like the last missing piece of the puzzle—the one that let it all finally come together.

Sweet smells fill the apartment: faken, warm maple syrup, and powdered sugar.

By the time we're all sitting down at the table together, talking and laughing, passing plates of food, no one is mad or scared or lonely or confused. Because we belong here with each other, and right now, that is enough.

I know that Gramps is not the same as he always was, and even if I catch glimpses now and then, he never will completely be his old self again. The thing is, I'm not the same as I was either. None of us are. But that's okay. More than okay: It's *serendipity*.

# Acknowledgments

\* \* \*

I started writing this book not long after I had to say good-bye to my sweet dog, Darwin. He was with me for twelve wonderful years, a constant source of love and companionship. Through both good times and bad, he was there, teaching me how to be a better, more loving person every day. I may have adopted him from the shelter, but he is the one who did all the rescuing in our relationship. And so this book has so much of his beautiful heart in its pages.

There were moments as I was writing this book—in 2020, a year like no other—when I thought I would never finish. Without the following people, I wouldn't have:

First, I thank YOU, yes *you*, dear readers, for joining me on this journey and inspiring me every step of the way. To the animal lovers out there who know the magic that happens between an animal and their special person. And to those of you who haven't yet had the honor, I hope you will someday.

To my agent, Jess Regel: Without you, this book would

quite literally not exist. Thank you for always helping me see the forest for the trees. You understood the true heart of this story before I did, and I cannot thank you enough for letting me in on the secret. I am the luckiest author in the world to have you and Helm Literary in my corner.

Heartfelt gratitude goes to my amazing editor, Ruta Rimas, for being my champion on this new middle grade leg of my writing journey. On our fourth book together, your thoughtful, sensitive editing continues to make me a better writer and storyteller. Your support, guidance, and insight have shaped this book in far too many ways to list here. "Thank you" does not begin to cover it, but a million times over, *thank you*.

Thanks are also due to Casey McIntyre, Gretchen Durning, Jessica Jenkins, Jayne Ziemba, Anna Elling, and the entire Razorbill team—so many talented, dedicated people had a hand in making this book a reality, and I am grateful to each and every one of you. Kelly Murphy, thank you for bringing the Code Name world to life through your incredible artwork—I can't help but smile every time I look at the cover.

My writer friends (aka the Camp Nebo crew), who are always there to lend an ear or shoulder along the way, I couldn't imagine doing this whole writing thing without each of you. Thanks also to the brilliant, talented authors who were generous enough to offer up their own words of endorsement: Jenn Bishop, Kathleen Burkinshaw, Gillian McDunn, Rebecca Petruck, and Megan Shepherd.

As always, I owe an enormous debt of gratitude to my friends and family. Especially my parents, Mary and Tim, who instilled in me a love and respect for animals early on. To all the fur babies who have come into my life, past, present, and future. And last but never least, thank you to my wife, Samantha—I could not do it (writing, life, anything) without you.